Wounds to Wishes

Tales of Mystery and Melancholy

Chad Lutzke, Robert Ford, and John Boden

Book 1 in Crystal Lake's Dark Tide series

Let the world know:
#IGotMyCLPBook!

Crystal Lake Publishing
www.CrystalLakePub.com

WELCOME
TO ANOTHER

CRYSTAL LAKE PUBLISHING
CREATION

Join today at www.crystallakepub.com & www.patreon.com/CLP

Subscribe to Crystal Lake Publishing's Dark Tide series for updates, specials, behind-the-scenes content, and a special selection of bonus stories - http://eepurl.com/hKVGkr

The Strangest Twist Upon Her Lips

CHAD LUTZKE

CHAPTER 1

I'M LYING IN the tub with Rita, holding her. It's freezing, and I haven't made the call. I'm taking my time, because this is the end of us, and I can't show up at her funeral. Her whole bitter family will lose their shit. So, this is my viewing. This is my visitation.

For one quick second, I worry about fingerprints, like I'll be blamed for what she did and the proof is on my hands. But then I realize how ridiculous that is and run a hand across her body. Her skin feels like clay. It doesn't feel like Rita anymore.

I've been lying in here with her, in this crimson bed of freezing slush, for at least an hour, and I think I'm done crying, like I've shed every fucking tear there is. Then I feel the knot in my throat—a fist that's slowly making its way up from my insides. And I bawl again. My face is tired from the strain, and I think about when parents teach their kids how their face will stay that way when they contort it. That's how my face feels, like it'll always be like this. And I'm convinced it will. A decade of wrinkles in a matter of an hour from grief alone. Deep valleys and crow's feet.

I'm annoyed with the sound of my own crying as it bounces off the tile walls—a constant weeping loop, making me feel even more alone, more pathetic.

I kiss Rita's clay lips and let her face sink back under water. I don't close her eyes because that's too final. I'm still in denial.

Her hair floats and sways—strawberry-blonde tendrils. Bubbles hit the surface, and I pretend she'd purposefully been holding that last bit of breath while I weep over her, wrapped around her, like Lennon around Yoko.

I stand up. My skin is gooseflesh, and my teeth clack and chatter like there's a fucking jackhammer in my mouth. My penis has never been this cold, this shrunken, like having retreated from the touch of Rita's stiffened leg.

I look down and I'm stained red from the water. There's blood on the side of the tub and on the floor I hadn't seen before. Before, when I walked in and found Rita, everything was a blur. An explosion of red on white. I remember nearly passing out. I don't remember taking my clothes off.

I grab my cell and finally make the call. When the woman on the other end asks for my address, I go blank. I'm thinking of old addresses. The one where I grew up with my parents, my grandmother's in Missouri, where I stayed during college, even the shit job I had scooping ice cream for two years to save for a car. They're all on the tip of my tongue.

"Sir?" she says, and it sounds like she's down a well. Or I am.

I apologize, then figure it out.

When I go to hang up, I wait for her to say, "I'm sorry for your loss," but she doesn't. I don't know what dispatch protocol is, but if it were me answering calls, I'd say it.

I've got blood all over me. None of it's on my clothes. That doesn't look good, so I grab a towel and wipe down, then get dressed and lean against the tub, getting blood on my shirt and on my knees, and I stick my arms in the water up to the elbows so it looks like I held her from the floor instead of stripping naked in a moment of desperate weakness, needing to hold her one last time. I wouldn't expect anyone to understand. I don't even understand. Grief, shock. They make a person do strange things, I guess. Ed Gein taught us that.

But I'm not Ed Gein. I'm Brenton Willard. And I don't rob graves and collect lady parts. I don't even miss my mom all that much. I just get naked to have one last quiet moment with my fiance, because she took that from us when she slit her wrists.

CHAPTER 2

I toss Rita's fix kit in the garbage. I don't want anyone finding it. There's nothing in it, hasn't been for two years now, but holding onto it kept her clean. Like a sober drunk with a bottle in the freezer. It's a security blanket.

I'm on the balcony, waiting for the ambulance or coroner or

whoever the hell they're sending, and the stars are out, and I can't for the life of me figure out why she did it. If she were ever going to kill herself, I'd think it would have been two years ago. We were getting married this summer. We were going to make love on the golf course at midnight and steal the golf carts and race from green to green until we got caught, then we'd run for the woods and to the car, where we'd parked beforehand. We were going to act like fools and be young again.

I can't figure it out. Not for the life of me.

An ambulance pulls up, followed by a police car. I picture a coroner next, with its sleek black paint, camouflaged and symbolic.

The cop is asking me questions while the paramedics stare at Rita, then they go in the hallway and talk. The questions are typical, obvious. I want to tell the cop to go fuck himself, that he should be able to figure out what the hell happened without drilling me.

The coroners walk in, and the cop moves out of the way. They have a gurney that folds. The cop points toward the bathroom, and it hits me that I'll never see Rita again. But I don't want to watch them pull her out of the tub. I don't want those images popping up on those too long nights while I'm trying to sleep.

I can hear the water splashing and the drain being pulled, and I'm not even listening to the cop anymore. I don't give a shit what he has to say.

Then he says, "I'm sorry for your loss," and he's holding a card in his hand with his name on it.

I take the card and put it in my pocket without even thinking.

"Did she leave a note?" the cop is asking me.

I tell him I didn't see one. But I didn't really look. I don't know if I want a note. I'm not sure I can handle it. And as soon as the cop nods at me, like maybe he's leaving now, I look at the coffee table and see an envelope with my name on it in pink marker. I quickly look away because I don't want the cop to see it. It's not for him. It's none of his business.

I watch the gurney go by, Rita cocooned in shiny black. My tongue hurts and I realize I'm biting it, trying not to cry. I just want this cop to get out of my face and these people to leave so I can scream and throw myself against the wall, maybe jump from the balcony. And I'll wonder what it's like for Rita now, and it doesn't matter if I ever believed in God before because I'm making up my mind right now that's where she is. In His arms. No more suffering.

Suffering? Suffering from what?

I try not to look at the letter again because the cop is still here. But I think about it. I think about what it says and how I can't handle it.

Finally, the paramedics in the hall leave, and I hear the coroners downstairs pushing the door open, maneuvering Rita through it, and the cop says something I can't hear, then turns to leave.

I wait until they're in their cars and vans and trucks, and I put a hole in the wall with my fist and another with my foot.

CHAPTER 3

I'm staring at the envelope with my name written in pink. It's in cursive, like there should be a heart next to it, filled in. I stare so long it's like I'm trying to read through the envelope. I want to grab it, throw it in the sink and douse it with lighter fluid set it aflame so it's not there to tempt me. Keeping it around like a bottle in the freezer won't bring me peace. It won't stop an urge. This isn't a security blanket. It's a fucking albatross.

I leave the envelope there and run to the bedroom. There's a cardboard box under the bed. I grab it, open it. This is like a movie now. The broken heart going through old memories, smiling, crying, laughing, raging, going through the stages. It's exactly what I do.

There's so many pictures to go through, but I want to savor them, so I only grab a small stack of about twenty. Most of them are from when we went downtown and took turns sitting on the lap of a statue. There's a picture of me dry humping it. Rita laughed so hard when I did that. We were both pretty high at the time.

I spot a folded piece of paper, unfold it. It's a bucket list I haven't seen in nearly four years. We put it together one night while high. We were neck-deep in addiction at the time. Two of the things at the top of the list are crossed off:

*Dine and ditch.

*Piss on a police car.

We'd gone to Ferg's on 28th and ordered lobster and crab and wine. We even asked for a doggie bag, but they wanted us to pay the bill first, so we ran. We ran like school kids ding-dong ditching, laughing our asses off on the way. We'd even constructed a plan ahead of time that we'd split up and meet at the park behind the yellow park bench. We didn't think of how full we'd be, and Rita puked on her way to the park from running.

For the police-car pissing, we saw one outside a Denny's. It was an easy in and out. Rita even participated. While I took the driver's side door, she squatted over the rear bumper. Piss went all down her leg and into her pants. We were laughing so hard I thought she might hyperventilate.

Most of the list is filled with shit we thought would make us feel like kids again, or make us feel good about ourselves, take away the reality that we were fucked up, that we'd wasted years wasting away. Staring at it, I'm full of regret that we never did the rest together. Maybe if we had, Rita wouldn't have left me like this. It's the first of a million what-ifs to come.

"Why didn't you tell me what was going on?" I say. And just like in the bathroom, the sound of my own voice makes me lonelier than ever.

I start to fear that I'll kill myself one day. Like our shared past, our shared present is some contagious ghost meant to harm, and I'm next. And suddenly, I have the strangest motivation to do everything on the list. I want to be able to cross out every crazy idea we'd written down. Not to stop the creeping death over my shoulder, but to feel close to Rita again, maybe even make her laugh from the clouds, to shake her head in teasing disbelief that I never forgot our list, and here I am actually doing it, checking the entries off, running from the trouble I've caused, and laughing.

As I gaze at the entries, considering each one of them, I realize the real reason for the desire is to avoid the letter and to avoid the trauma of the whole evening.

I look at the clock. It's 6:00 p.m. Fuck it.

Buy a bird and set it free.
I drink a cup of coffee, then grab my keys.

Rita and I had talked about what kind of bird. I remember her saying, "It can't be just any bird. Some can't survive on their own."

This entry on the list makes more sense than the others. I think it was symbolic of our own freedom we wanted so badly at the time. When you've got a needle in your arm, there are only two things you want in the world: To never come down. And to never have the desire to do it again.

I drive to Bo's Pet World, and I can't believe I'm out in the world already and not curled up in bed, crying myself to sleep that'll never come. I mean, I just found my fiancé dead, and I'm going to the fucking pet store to buy a bird. Every car that passes feels like an opportunity to crash, and even though I don't want to die, I'm preoccupied with the thought that the ideation will suddenly tap on my shoulder so hard I'll veer into oncoming traffic, crashing through the windshield and landing on the hood of someone's car—an image the other driver only shares with their shrink once a week for the next decade.

The sign on the door tells me the pet store closes in half an hour. The birds are the first thing I hear when I walk in. Macaws and parrots in the back. Two of them aren't even caged. I'm not sure they're for sale, could be mascots, like a cat in an old bookstore, lounging on the counter all day.

I see the ringneck doves, two of them, cozying up to one another. These are the ones Rita said we should buy.

"Excuse me, ma'am."

The salesperson is the first woman I've talked to since Rita died, and I feel a strange guilt creep in, like I'm doing something wrong. I tell the woman I want the two doves. They look like they're in love.

She tells me they make wonderful pets and asks if I need help picking out a cage because they have some on sale. I tell her no. I lie and say I already have everything I need, except food. I'm worried the birds won't find food when I let them go, so I buy a bag.

She keeps trying to upsell me like she only gets paid commission. As kindly as I can, I tell her for the third time that all I need are the birds and the bag of food, then we're at the checkout, and she shows me a magazine with birds on the cover and says, "There's a great article on ringnecks in here." I lie again and tell her I already have it, just to shut her up. I don't think she believes me, but she finally takes the hint.

I'm walking to my car and see a tent pitched across the street. It's next to a TV repair place. There's a shopping cart filled with shit nearby. A homeless person lives there, probably a junkie.

I'm tempted to let the doves go right there by my car, but a parking lot is no kind of home, so I hop in the car, put them in the backseat, and drive to the park. I can hear the doves cooing. It's like they're having a conversation, wondering what the next chapter in their short lives holds. I wish Rita could hear it. She would cry. Happy endings always made her cry.

It's 74 degrees out, still, quiet, getting dark. And I take the birds over behind the yellow bench where Rita and I ran after filling up on lobster and crab and wine. I don't throw the doves in the air because I don't want them to split apart. Instead, I set them on the ground and pour the food out. They're walking around, not that interested in the food. I name one of the birds Rita and the other Brenton.

They won't stop walking around, like they haven't figured out they're free. Maybe they've never even flown before. Maybe they've been sitting in that fucking cage their whole life, conversing, cozying, falling in love.

I'm watching these birds for 10 minutes, 20 minutes, and I start crying because they just don't get it. They don't have to be walking around on the ground anymore. I start to wonder if they're not flying because it's dark and maybe I should have waited, but then they take off together, and it's so dark I can't even watch them go. They just disappear, and I'm reminded of how I couldn't say goodbye to Rita.

But they're free now.

I pretend Rita is dancing on a cloud, not looking down from afar seeing the doves' freedom on a giant HD flatscreen, picking up every detail, and the camera is following these birds, and she's crying because she's so happy, and maybe that bucket list isn't so crazy after all.

Steal from the rich and give to the poor

I'm not sure how to go about this one, so I sit on the yellow bench and think on it. A couple walk by holding hands, and it breaks my heart. I feel for the suicide letter in my pocket. I don't know why I brought it with me. I still won't read it. Maybe it *is* a security blanket. I wonder if it'll be a permanent part of my pants now, like a belt, guitar pick, or wallet, just sitting in there flattened, the envelope slowly flaking away at the creases.

I remember my boss is away on vacation. He's a dirtbag, the

kind who cuts corners. Safety comes last and so do raises. I know where he lives because he had a Christmas party there one year. I think he wanted to show off the pool and the Porsche and the library filled with books he's never read: Tolstoy and Dante and Nietzsche and other bullshit he thinks makes him look like an intellectual.

I hop in the car and head for Candlewood. I picture Rita sitting in the passenger seat, chugging an energy drink and shouting "We Are 138" by The Misfits, getting pumped. This is what she'd do.

My boss, Jim Embleton, his front lawn is glowing with floodlights. I'll bet his neighbors hate him. He's their constant nightlight, Venetian shadows painted on their bedroom walls while they try and sleep. I have no idea if he has an alarm system.

I tuck my hair under my hat and keep my head down, following the line of hedges that wrap the house. I'm making my way to the backyard, which is only partially lit by a single spotlight. There are two windows in the darkest part of the yard. I check them. They're both locked. I keep close to the house and check the back door. It's locked. I check the garage door. It's unlocked. Dumbass.

This is where the Porsche is parked. It's got a black tarp over it that fits like a tight pair of leather pants. The other parking space is empty. They took his wife's vehicle.

Along the back wall are totes. Everything is organized, labeled. I go for the door into the house. It's locked. I'm about to push my elbow through the window when I see a red tool chest. It's shiny like it's brand new. I pull the drawers. Every tool inside is oil-free and shines like the moon on the crest of a wave. Everything is new, unused. Just like the library books. The asshole doesn't even need these tools.

I grab the tarp from the Porsche and pull it off, then fill the tarp with tools I think are the most expensive. I grab the sides of the tarp and cinch it over my shoulder like some giant bag Santa might carry, and head back to the car.

I'm in the car, rubbing my shoulder. It's sore as hell from lugging the tools. I feel my belly for a hernia. I'm not familiar with them, have no idea what they feel like, but I know it's like your guts trying to find a way out through your stomach. I'm being ridiculous. I'm fine.

The tools I lifted will be worth something to someone. I decide I'm gonna take them to the pawn shop in the morning, first thing.

Mr. Embleton will notice the tarp missing right away, but he won't notice the tools are gone for at least a year. Fucking poser.

CHAPTER 4

I'm at home on the couch, and it hits me hard that Rita is gone. She made herself go. It's over. Tackling the bucket list took my mind off things. I didn't feel young, but I did feel alive. And now I've got this survivor's guilt going on. She should be here, freeing birds and stealing for the poor.

This is the worst day of my life.

My head is in this strange place, where I feel like I'm watching myself, like I'm in a movie and there should be a soundtrack. A different album for each phase. Slayer's Reign in Blood for my rage, Black Flag's My War side two for the pathetic misery, and Journey's Greatest Hits for the quiet moments and for the hopeful ones. If they ever come.

I walk into the bathroom to shut the light off because I'm finally tired and headed for bed. I've forgotten about the blood. It's still there. I want to clean it up so the stark reminder is gone, but it's the last part of Rita I'll ever see again.

I grab the whitest towel I can find, a newer one Rita bought because she loves the feel of a virgin towel—before any bleach or detergent hit it, before the fibers are flattened like a kitchen rug—and I wipe down the floor and the tub, then I rinse the tub out. The towel is crimson now. I fold it and set it on the floor next to the toilet. I'll never wash it.

I'm exhausted. The crying, the cleaning, the grieving, and the rush of tool-stealing adrenaline are like a tranquilizer. I throw myself in our bed and feel the emptiness next to me, pretending, at the very least, there's a ghost there who wishes it could speak.

CHAPTER 5

I'm wide awake. It's been four hours. There's no way I'm getting back to sleep. It's like I drank a pot of coffee. I hit the bathroom and brush my foot against the towel while I pee. This will become a ritual, I'm sure of it.

I need to hit a meeting. I can feel the unexpected pull of the needle. It comes out of nowhere, like a bat loose in the house, wings fluttering in sporadic, unpredictable patterns. If I don't act now, it could get me.

The first morning meeting isn't for three more hours.

When you're on the junk, you're waiting to die. You know it's inevitable, but you just don't care. You've been re-wired, and the innocence and morality you once held has been dissolved by the contents of a dirty spoon. It takes some time being clean before the wiring repairs itself, and sometimes it never does. Some find themselves in a world of paranoia and delusions they can't escape, the wiring is so knotted. I start to entertain the idea that I've never used H as a means for escaping grief and maybe it could help, but immediately I recognize the building of an excuse. I see the pieces coming together like a stairway to relapse, each step a lie to the next.

I pull the bucket list and the letter from my pocket and set them on the table side by side like two bullets being readied for a game of Russian roulette. One or both hold freedom. One or both hold my potential downfall.

I grab the list.

Lay flowers on one hundred graves

I drive to the supermarket that's open all night. I buy every carnation they have. Red, pink, yellow, white, blue. They run out. I buy daises and black-eyed susans to make up the difference. I walk out with one-hundred flowers in a shopping cart.

"She must be somebody special," a woman says with a smile.

The car reeks of flowers. Too much of a good thing. I drive to Lakewood Memorial because I know they don't have a gate they close at night. Some of the people were buried there last century, some last week.

I put flowers on the smallest gravesites. I put them on the

biggest. Women, children, men. Each time I lay one down, I say the person's name and give a little nod. After a few dozen, it starts to feel obsessive, but I know it's what Rita would have done.

I finally get through all one-hundred flowers, and I'm beat. I sit down on the edge of the fountain in the middle of the cemetery. The sun is just starting to come up, painting the tips of the tallest stones and mausoleums. It's a beautiful place, and I'm hoping Rita's parents will put her here. Them hating me has made this even more difficult. We should be together during this time. But I know they'll blame me, just like they blamed me for her drug use. I don't even know how to tell them. I figure I'll tell Rita's brother, and he can relay it. He seems to hate me least.

As the sun shows itself, I can see the flowers better, peppered throughout like candy sprinkles on a dew-laced cupcake made of grass. I bow my head and say a little prayer for everyone, but especially for Rita.

CHAPTER 6

I find out the pawn shop opens early and decide to go there before I hit a meeting. But first, I transfer the tools into some cardboard boxes. I don't want to drag the tarp in there, looking even more conspicuous, like some junkie hauling hot goods. Or an ex-junkie hauling hot goods.

My phone rings. It's Bobby, my old sponsor. He still keeps tabs on me. I answer. He can tell right away something's wrong. The guy knows me better than anyone, except for Rita.

"What's going on, Brenton?"

"Just heading out, thinking about hitting an eight o'clock."

"Sounds good. Now what's *really* going on?"

I manage not to break down while telling him about Rita. He knew her pretty well too.

"Oh shit, man. I'm coming over."

"I won't be here. Meet me at the eight?"

"Okay, yeah. Definitely. You make sure you get your ass there. Promise me."

"I will. Promise."

The pawnshop reeks of cigarettes and motor oil. A zit-covered teen stands behind the counter next to a man I assume is his dad. They both sport the same greasy red hair. The man is obese and wears denim overalls that dig into his shoulders. There's a cigarette burning in a tin ashtray in front of him.

"I've got some tools if you're interested," I say.

He sees the box in my arms and clears the counter off to make room. "Let's see what you got."

I tell him I have more in the car.

"Well . . . let's get 'em all in here then."

I set the box on the counter and grab the others.

He's looking over them, picks one up, eyes it, eyes me. "Decided you're not the working-man type, eh?" He's waiting for a reply. "It's just, these tools look pretty new. Where'd you get 'em?"

"My father-in-law. He thinks I'm some kind of mechanic."

"Doesn't have his own son to pass 'em down to, huh?"

"Right."

He knows they're stolen. He deals with hot shit all day.

"What are you lookin' to get for 'em?"

"Whatever's fair," I say.

He tugs at his overalls and the straps dig further into him. "I'll give you one-fifty for everything."

"Okay."

He seems surprised I don't haggle. "Alright then. I just need you to sign this . . . " He slides a little book across the counter and hands me a pen. What I scribble isn't decipherable. It's not even English, just a mess of lines. I cross a T and dot an I that isn't really there to make it look good. He opens the drawer and counts out one-hundred and fifty dollars. "Come on back if your father-in-law keeps gifting you shit you can't use." He winks.

I hit the McDonald's across the street and grab a dozen breakfasts, including one for myself. Hashbrowns, egg McMuffins, sausage. I walk down Capital Street and hand the food out to the homeless, along with a little money.

One woman is with her four-year-old daughter. She starts crying when I hand her two bags and some bills.

"I'm no beggar, sir. It's just . . . it all happened so fast, you know?" She takes the bags and looks at her daughter, who could use a brush to her hair and some decent sleep, judging by the purple under her eyes. "Tell the nice man, thank you."

The girl shies away and hides in her mother's arm. I can't imagine the shit she's seen.

Once the food is gone, I head to the eight o'clock meeting.

Bobby's there when I pull up, standing outside smoking a cigarette. He's a bear of a man, not necessarily tall, just wide, big bones and big gut, big beard that hides his big chin. He greets me at the car when I get out, gives me a hug. I break down.

"I'm so sorry, man," he says. "Life just ain't fair, brother. But I'm glad you're here. This is where you belong." He's squeezing me tight like I can barely breathe, and his belly is pushing into me like a knotted tree trunk.

"I can't read the letter, Bobby." I'm crying into his shoulder.

"There ain't no hurry. You do it when you're ready, and if that means never . . . that's okay."

Suddenly, the idea of never reading what Rita left feels like an unforgivable sin, like a huge middle finger to her grave. The words she wrote were some of the last through her mind. They're from a deep place I've never seen. I imagine they're full of about as much truth as someone can offer. That truth may be ugly, it may be brutal, but it's honest. And that's all we'd ever asked from one another.

I let go of Bobby and wipe my face on my sleeve. He grips my shoulder and gives it a squeeze. "You're gonna be fine, my friend. A lesser man would have already grabbed the poison."

I muster a smile and thank him.

"Now, if you take up cigarettes again, can't say I blame you." He lets out a big belly laugh that's contagious, and I sniffle through one myself.

I see all the familiar faces. Chuck sitting at the head of the far table, like always, lips pursed over a game of solitaire, arthritic hands flipping the next three cards.

Danni is talking to a long-haired kid I've never seen before. She's got her flirt turned on. I don't doubt the kid will find himself in her bed soon enough.

Lance and Landon are sitting behind their Styrofoam cups, playing Gin-Rummy. Landon sees me and offers a wave and a smile.

There's a dozen others drinking coffee, reading, staring off.

I sit down, and Bobby joins me. The meeting starts, and I don't recognize the person chairing it. I realize it's been a while. Maybe too long. I found out years ago, during a relapse, it's never a good idea to stay away from the tables for too long. But under the circumstances, I'm surprised I'm here. If Bobby hadn't called, maybe I wouldn't be.

I listen to a woman talk about her daughter who just started going to raves. Her daughter thinks the drugs she takes are good for her, opening her mind. She's sleeping around a lot, was even arrested in a parking lot for getting nailed against a car by two guys high on molly. I feel bad for the mother. It's tough as shit watching someone you love waste away. Youth and the fog of drugs don't mix well.

After the meeting, I'm talking to Bobby, and he's telling me about his psychologist. He's telling me about how much it's helped him. "These tables . . . they can only do so much. Something like what you're going through, I'd think about seeing someone."

I tell him I'll look into it. I don't have so much pride I can't warm a couch for an hour and talk about the dark shit.

CHAPTER 7

I spend the rest of the day cleaning the apartment, organizing, giving in to crying fits, and watching hours of reruns I can't pay attention to. I think about hitting another meeting just to pass the time and to be in the presence of anyone at all. But somehow, I manage to take a nap, only to wake up with the haunting reminder of how life has changed.

I start to send Rita's brother a text message, then stop. What kind of bullshit pussy move is that? You don't text something like this. I dial his number. He picks up on the second ring, way too early. I have no idea what to say.

"Hey, Jerry . . . It's Brenton."

There's silence, then, "Is Rita okay?"

He knows I'd have no other reason to call. The hate from her family is cinder-block strong, and I can hear in Jerry's voice that it may have been reinforced since we last spoke.

"Actually . . . no, man. She's not."

"The fuck did you do?"

I've never touched Rita in any way that wasn't gentle. Jerry's hate, the distrust and paranoia, they come from my past with drugs. What he doesn't know . . . what he'll never know, is Rita started first. Trying heroin was her idea. She took that first step. And I followed.

What else the family doesn't know is what I went through to get her clean after I finally did, being with her every second of the way, through those long, sweat-filled nights where she'd beg me for a fix, and we'd cry together for hours. I'd preach everything I ever heard at the meetings, every scripture I could remember, even if it had nothing to do with what she was going through. And my favorite: *"Tough times never last, but tough people do."* I must have said that a dozen times during that first night of agony.

"I didn't do anything, Jerry," I say. "She did. She . . . "

"She left you, and now you're looking for her? Well, guess what, dickhead. You're calling the wrong guy, because if I find out she's running from you, I'm heading straight to your place and fucking your world up. You hear me?"

It sounds like I'd have been better off calling Rita's mom. Someone got to Jerry, strengthened that ire. The last time we talked was on Rita's birthday. He came over to drop off a gift, and we had a beer together. Didn't exactly break bread, but it was civil, and I thought he'd torn down the wall enough to see I wasn't the monster his family portrayed me as.

There's no getting out of the rest of the phone call. No one but me knows Rita is dead. I have to say something.

"Jerry . . . Rita's dead."

"The fuck did you say?"

"She killed herself . . . "

There's silence, then an explosion of insults and threats and disbelief. I finally get a small window to speak and give him the same info the cop gave me: where she is now and what their next step should be. His rant is so extreme, I have to shout in the phone how sorry I am, then hang up.

If the family hated me before, I'm now at the top of their kill list. I won't be surprised if her brother comes over in a drunken stupor with a baseball bat in hand.

My phone rings, but I ignore it and go to the closet, grab my gun. Rita hated that I had it. But after we got clean, some of the old crowd were showing up, peering through the windows, spraying graffiti on the building, leaving needles around. People don't like it when you get clean. Misery loves company and all that. And if they think you've got money, and they know the layout of your house, chances are good they'll try and break in. Since we weren't allowed to have a dog, the gun was our protection. I'd even gotten a license to carry but never took it outside the apartment. Not until today.

It takes me a minute to figure out how to work the holster. After I've got it strapped on, I head outside. My phone is still blowing up, and I know Jerry will be heading over. I don't want to be here when he shows.

Spend a night with the homeless

I'm killing two birds here. Staying away from my house for a day or two is a good idea, and it's the perfect time to tackle the next entry on our list.

Rita and I often talked about being homeless. It was our biggest fear, and it always felt like we were on the verge of it, living in a cardboard box with every fix. We lucked out, and that never happened. But we'd seen it happen to friends of ours. Good people who went off the deep end even more than we were. Like my friend Matthew. He was prescribed Norco after tearing a ligament playing football with his kid. These doctors, they hand that shit out to anyone, knowing what the outcome can be. I've seen honor-roll kids get a root canal, and two years down the road they're in the alley on their knees for some meth or H or crack.

With Matthew, he was a family man, worked as a pharmacy tech. But after getting hooked on Norco was fired from his job for stealing it when he'd ran through his script too fast. A lot of these people, they find out how much cheaper H is, so they'll settle for that. Once that happens, it's all over. Matthew died in the basement of a squat house with a needle in his arm, naked and full of sores, smelling like shit. It's miracle when someone can find the strength to walk away. That's what Rita and I were, a pair of miracles.

I head downtown to the park—the weeping willows, the pond, and the benches. They're an ugly oil painting with a gaudy frame. The scene brings back memories I'd rather not remember. We never slept overnight here, but we scored and booted surrounded by these trees and these dirty tents.

There must be twenty tents scattered throughout the park, with trash bags and duffel bags and shopping carts parked next to them. People of varying races and sexes waste away here. Hard drugs don't give a fuck who you are.

I sit in the grass next to the pond. The water is full of wrappers floating on the surface. I see a few empty bottles down under, one of them is broken. The city has given up on this place. It's like its own little village where its leader packed their bags and made for greener pastures. There's just anarchy now.

Despite my somber surroundings, I get the sudden urge to use—roll up my sleeve and bury a needle. To fight the craving, I think about a woman who spoke at this morning's meeting. She didn't say her name, just, "Hi . . . I'm an addict," like nothing else mattered, like her only identity was an ugly past. I'd never seen her before, and I probably won't again because of the bomb she dropped on the group. The kind of story you tell once and move on because you're afraid you've ruined any chance of making friends.

She was talking about how she was babysitting for her sister while high. This kid, her two-year-old nephew, was screaming for food, just going off and chanting "Hungry! Hungry!" while beating on the side of the oven with the flat of his hand. And this woman. This no-named woman, she was boiling hot dogs after having just loaded up. And when she pulled the pan off the stove she just froze there, peaking, nodding. Then she dropped the pan of boiling water on this two-year-old kid who's slamming his hand on the side of the oven. The woman didn't even know she dropped it, didn't feel it leave her hand. She said the kid's screams were silent, like there was just too much pain to make a sound, like the kid drew a gasp so deep, so intense that nothing came out until he drew another breath. That's when the woman snapped out of it. She said she quit using that very day but hasn't spoken to her sister since.

I sit and think about her and how bad things get when you're using and how it isn't just you you're affecting. It's everyone around you. Even complete strangers. These thoughts help stave the craving.

I make my way to the far side of the park, where a line of bushes cover a chain-link fence, which helps hide the ugly eyesore that is the back of a plaza painted like tan flesh. There's an old woman sitting outside her tent, must be in her 60s, maybe 70s. She's wearing a long raincoat and has hair like a Brillo pad with bits of leaf stuck in it. She's sitting cross-legged with a paperback book in her lap. I'm a pretty good judge of character, and I don't think this woman has touched drugs in her life. Not everyone here is a practicing addict. Some of them are veterans, some suffer from mental illness with no family to watch over them. I could tell that was probably her case.

I get closer and see that the book is *Stranger in a Strange Land* by Heinlein. I sit down next to her, but not too close. I don't want to spook her. She's probably used to having her shit stolen. She doesn't move, doesn't look up.

"Ever read Asimov?" I say.

She puts a finger in the book, closes it, looks me up and down. "Read the Foundation trilogy three times so far." I can see she's got a few teeth missing in front, causing a slight whistle when she talks. "You read sci-fi I take it?"

"No, but I had a roommate who did. His favorite was Asimov. Used to see the books around the apartment."

"Bet he read that Star Wars bullshit too, huh?"

I smile. "Actually, he did."

"So . . . what's your story?" she says. "You don't look like a junkie."

"Used to be."

"You don't look homeless either."

"I'm not."

"You here to tell me about Jesus or somethin'?"

I like this woman. She's spry, witty. I can't imagine the stories she has. Rita would have liked her too. "No . . . nothing like that. To be honest, I'm not sure why I'm sitting here."

"Well, it sure as hell can't be cuz you're looking for a piece of ass." She leans back, gives me a side-eye. "Unless old ladies is your kink."

"You've given up on people, haven't you?"

"How's that?" she says.

"Because you don't think a person can sit next to you and strike up a conversation without wanting something."

"You *do* want something. You want me to either kill your boredom or your curiosity." She looks at me with gray eyes, a sort of twinkle in them. "Am I wrong?"

"No, I guess you're not. You know . . . you're too smart to be living in a tent."

She sets the book down next to her in the dirt-grass. "People who think they know everything are a great annoyance to those of us who do."

"I've heard that before."

"Asimov said it."

"Sounds like he thought highly of himself."

"He was an arrogant ass. He also said, 'For whatever the tortures of Hell, I think the boredom of Heaven would be even worse.'"

"Sounds like he took them old paintings a little too literal, the ones with the naked baby-angels floatin' in the clouds," I say.

"Exactly. But even then, I'd rather stare at a kid's ass all day than deal with the fire and the brimstone. You know what that shit smells like? Rotten eggs. Like someone shit their drawers. No thank you."

I start to laugh, and then guilt swoops in like a seagull snatching a bite of sandwich from my mouth, like I have no business enjoying life anymore. "So, what's your story? . . . If you don't mind me asking."

"Oh dear . . . I don't think you have the time. Long story short, I'm what the state deems clinically insane. Spent a few years in the hospital, and when I got out, my husband was gone, took every bit of my life with him."

"That's why you're homeless?"

"Yessir. And before you ask why can't I get a job, it's cuz I see shit that ain't there." She brushes at her hair with her fingers, picks at a few leaves and discards them.

"You seem pretty normal to me."

"That's because I'm drunk off my ass." She cackles when she says it. "It's the only thing that helps."

"I suppose you've tried medication."

"Dear . . . there ain't a pill I haven't tried."

"I'm not trying to be preachy or anything, but you ever consider alcohol being the culprit?"

"The last time I went a day without drinking, I took a shit in the middle of the road because I thought someone told me to. The same someone who told me to try and claw the cop's eyes out who was reprimanding me for said shit. Trust me, the world is a safer place when I'm at least half a bottle deep."

I doubt alcohol is helping balance her mental health. If anything, it's making things worse, but I leave it alone, change the subject. "Where's the safest spot to sleep in the park?"

She gives me a confused look. "I thought you said you wasn't homeless?"

"I'm not. Call it a social experiment."

"You wanna see what it feels like."

"Something like that," I tell her.

"You tell anyone else around here that, you might find yourself with a broken face and your shoes missing."

"Probably. Hope I didn't offend you." Then, without even thinking, I tell her everything. "My fiance killed herself yesterday. She left me a note, and I'm too chickenshit to read it. I'm sleeping in the park because we wrote a bucket list while high on dope, and the only thing I can think to do is do everything on it . . . for the both of us."

"Oh dear . . . Well, that explains things. You ain't got your head on right."

"No, I really don't."

She reaches out, touches my knee, pats it. "I'm sorry."

I start crying, but I don't let her see. I'm sure she knows, though. I'm sure she can feel it. Sometimes that's all it takes is to be near someone to know they're crying, like when you can tell an old television set is on in the next room.

"You're going to have to read that note sometime."

"Am I? What if I don't? What if I just hold onto it forever?"

I think she starts hearing those voices of hers because she looks away from me and says, "Oh, I'm not going to tell him that."

I wait, afraid I might embarrass her if I say something.

"No . . . that's nonsense. It's that kind of logic that gets me in trouble. Now, you mind your own business and leave the advice to me." She looks back at me. "Sorry . . . now, if you don't read it, you'll never be able to move on. That thing will haunt you. It's best to get it over with."

It's good advice, but I find myself wondering what the other advice is, what the voices told her.

"What's the other advice?" I ask.

Her eyes turn to slits. Her lips tighten. "Don't you pay any mind to that, dear. I'm just a crazy, old lady. Do you have the note with you?" It feels like she's asking if I'm holding a bag of stolen diamonds, something valuable she means to steal, and an irrational distrust flows through me.

"Yeah."

"Do you want me to read it to you?"

I laugh like it's the most absurd thing I've ever heard—a stranger offering to peek at the most private part of my life. "No," I tell her, and I reach to my back pocket, dip my fingers into the denim and feel the envelope's edges, making sure it's there, safe and secure.

I get the conversation back on the rails. "So, where do you recommend I sleep tonight? I mean . . . is there a particular spot that's safest . . . maybe more private?"

"Sorry, dear. It's a roll of the dice. There ain't no safe space. But you're welcome to hang around here. I won't take a shit on you or nothin'."

"Is that a thing?"

"You'd be surprised. I seen a few guys out here having piss fights, pissin' on each other's tents like they was dogs markin' territory."

"Okay . . . I trust you."

"As you should," she says. "And don't think a girl can't take a whiz on stuff, because she can. You just got to know how to aim is all."

I think of Rita pissing on the cop car, laughing uncontrollably, wetting herself. My stomach fills with lead from the memory.

The woman turns her head away from me. "Nope. Not a chance." She's talking to the voices again. "You can tempt me all you want. That ain't no task for him. That's our problem, not his."

Again, I wait for her to bring the conversation back my way, get past her episode. A few moments later she reaches out and pats my leg. "Anyway, not to worry, dear. I do my business in that dumpster over there." She points to an old, rusted dumpster behind the plaza.

"I'm not worried."

She holds a bony finger up that resembles a twig. "I've got a pillow for you." She peeks inside her tent, reaches an arm in, and pulls out a small pillow that looks like it used to be pink but has been bleached by the sun. It's crushed velvet–or used to be–something left from the 70s, with the velvet having been crushed beyond texture. Now it's just a stuffed, off-white cloth with missing patches here and there like a short-haired dog with a case of mange. "It don't look like much, but it's lice free and it's a lot softer than your elbow."

I take the pillow and thank her, then make myself comfortable, feeling for the gun through my jacket, when something soft hits my arm. A small pack of tissue.

"In case you need to dump," the woman says, then coughs and spits something solid a good eight feet from us. "Well . . . here's to sweet dreams. Don't let the bed bugs bite."

When she says the last little bit it has a child-like mischief behind it, like any second now she'll be giggling at a whoopie cushion she'd set in my pillow.

As I hug myself and drift off to sleep, I half-listen to the mumbling conversation she has with someone who isn't there.

CHAPTER 8

I wake up feeling like I can't breathe, like I'm suffocating. When I open my eyes, all I see is the face of the old woman. She has a drinking straw in her mouth, with the other end in my nose. I push her away and lean on my elbow. My sinuses feel like I've snorted chili powder, and I sneeze violently while my eyes tear up. My throat burns and my mouth tastes of clove and something bitter, like dandelion stems.

"What the fuck did you do?"

"I'm only trying to help, young man. Prepare for your vision quest."

"What?!" I'm doing my best to blow the shit from my nose, and she starts going on about how this is what I need and that I'll find the answers if I just let myself go. I'm half-listening.

"You crazy bitch!"

"I was afraid of this," she says. "You can't go in with a closed mind. You'll be more lost than ever."

For one quick moment, I worry that she's taken the note, that she's taken the gun. I check for both. They're still on me. But so are an abundance of feathers—gray, purple, white—scattered across my legs and in the grass around me. Next to my leg is a pigeon with its head tossed back and its tiny throat slit.

I stand and run through the park, away from her and her shaman voodoo bullshit.

"Open your mind!" she calls out behind me. "Follow the guide and find your way!"

Colors don't feel right, like I'm looking through a filter. And everything is far brighter than it should be, like the sun is made of fluorescent and it's just over my shoulder instead of barely peeking above the horizon.

The people I pass are faceless. Walking mannequins, driving mannequins. But not voiceless. Every head I see has sound coming from it. "Open your mind and find your way," they're saying. All using the same voice.

Nothing is how it should be, and I'm on the verge of panic. I break into a sprint, running through scenery that looks cartoonish. And I'm screaming, but I can't tell if any sound is coming out. The faceless voices are too loud. Or maybe it's too quiet and their voices are only in my head.

My face feels like it's covered in ice, then fire. Sweat (or tears) soak my face and it itches, like feathers being brushed against me with each bead of sweat that trails.

Out of nowhere, I recall a memory that feels more like a dream. A memory of a dream. I tilt my head back and stare at the dark blue sky, and the more I think on the memory I'm convinced it's a dream. And this memory-dream has me angrier than I've ever been in my life.

I've woke up horny before, rock hard. I've woke up sad, missing someone from a dream I never even met. But I've never woke up angry. This dream (memory?) has me seeing red, like I'm ready to put my fist through a wall of teeth, swell shut the first set of eyes I see. The rage has my stomach roiling, my heart racing. And the more I dwell on the memory-dream, the more the rage builds.

I try and focus on my surroundings and can make out a man

on a bicycle. His face is full of terror. "Boy, you done fucked up now!" He rides away so fast his feet slip off the pedals, trying to gain speed.

The anger I feel is incredible, and my whole body burns. Not a painful burn but like I'm wearing too many clothes, like I'm in the desert midday, the sun kicking my ass.

"What the fuck!" The words fly out of my mouth like a sneeze I can't hold back. It feels good somehow.

I think back to the dream/memory. It's about Rita's co-worker. A woman I've never met before, don't know her name. Not even sure she's real. In the dream/memory, Rita complained about her, said she got her fired, said this woman hated her because of her past.

While I work through the thoughts, my feet move me forward. I know exactly where I'm going. I'm heading to where Rita worked last year. But it doesn't feel like a conscious decision, and I don't even care because I'm so pissed off. There's another emotion there, too. No, not an emotion, a motive. It feels familiar, like the time in high school when I blackened that kid's eye after he tripped my friend in the hall. Or the time my stepdad hit my mom, so I put roadkill in his glovebox. Revenge. The familiar motive is revenge, and my feet are taking me to it.

～⌘～

I don't even use my car. It's not part of this rage-fueled equation. I walk a mile down Levington, then take a right onto Walnut. I'm thinking about this woman Rita talked about. This no-faced, no-named woman who got Rita fired. My mind is filled with entitlement I've never felt before, like this nameless bitch owes me because she was somehow the catalyst for Rita's suicide.

The sun is up. It's early, and I see the building where Rita worked, and I'm heading for the parking garage on the corner of Walnut and 2nd. I pull the gun from my waistband and feel the rubber grip against my palm, the cold steel against my fingers. This isn't like me at all. I'm not an evil man, but I've had evil thoughts. Just like everyone.

Evil thoughts like when a man once told Rita, "I'd love to eat that pussy." while she was pumping gas. In my head, that guy was on the ground, bleeding through every orifice in his head—the aftermath of jackhammering fists. Or the time I saw a father yank his kid by the arm, dragging him across a parking lot, skinning his knees all to hell. In my head, I beat the fuck out of that man while his kid watched.

We all get these thoughts. It's acting on them that makes you evil.

And I'm getting ready to act on one.

I put the gun inside my jacket and have a quick moment of focus as I reflect on waking up with a dead pigeon by my side, covered in feathers, finding myself in such an intense state of ire, and I sense something isn't right. But my mind fights the rationale and breaks free from questions I should be asking, like the guy who can't see past his own raging boner, only one thing on his mind.

I walk through the parking garage and take the stairs. I'm climbing them, paying no mind how many floors I'm going up, just watching my feet take each step, like a bored kid gazing at corn rows while passing them by on a road trip through the country with his parents.

Then my hand reaches for a door, and I swing it open. Right there in front of me is a woman. My mind tells me it's her. This is the bitch who hated Rita and got her fired.

I pull the gun out. "Gimme your fuckin' purse, bitch."

The voice doesn't even sound like mine. It's full of rasp and dirt roads, rusty hinges and broken bones. I'm two different people. There's the real me hidden deep inside with my jaw open, my eyes wide, yelling: *What the fuck are you doing, asshole?* Then there's the one with revenge on his mind based on a memory that might not even be real.

This woman, she clenches her purse. She's not giving it up. She's not scared. She's had enough shit from someone else, something else.

"I said, gimme your fuckin' purse!" I've got the gun in her face, and she's looking straight at me, deep into my eyes like she damn well knows I'm full of shit.

"No," she says.

"Fuck you say to me?" Inside, I'm kicking, I'm screaming *This isn't me!* I yell at her again, threaten to put a bullet in her.

"Then do it."

I hold the gun out, closer to her.

"Lady, I will *fuck* you up if—"

"You're *not* getting my purse, so either pull the trigger or don't pull the trigger, but quit wasting my time."

The real me deep inside is reveling in her resistance, cheering for her. But my arm reaches out like I'm a marionette hooked to strings calling the shots and reaches for her purse. She turns away quicker than I can get to it. Good for her.

"I said *no*," she says.

I scream at her. There's so much rage in my voice I can feel my eyes bulge as the words fly. "You crazyass bitch, I will fucking—"

"Then fucking do it!" She steps closer and puts her head against the barrel of the gun.

The real me has a moment of strength, and I turn from her. But my jacket gets caught on the door handle, and I lose my balance, drop the gun, and stumble down the steps, crashing hard against the wall.

When I look up, she's got the gun. I stand up, hold my empty hands out in surrender. The anger is gone now, leaving me with unspeakable shame. I mumble some words, trying to talk my way out of this. She raises the gun, and my throat fills with sand. I push off from the wall and run down the stairs, jumping each flight, pissing my pants on the way, filling them with a warm fear that will soon turn cold. Before I realize it, I'm on the first floor and through the door.

CHAPTER 9

Whether it be the realization of what I've done, the adrenaline-laced fear from nearly being shot, or because that shit up my nose has worn off, the anger is completely gone. Every irrational thought has disappeared, and I'm me again—the lonely guy searching for answers as to why his girl left, not just him, but her place in the world.

It takes me a moment to remember where I am and which direction is home. I want to head back to the park and ask just what in the hell that schizo witch thought she was doing. But my expectations are low. I'll get no answers. She's nuts.

My legs burn from the run here, and I have a hard time

remembering how I even got to the parking garage. And when I reflect, picturing myself running down the street, filled with blind rage, it's in third person, like the whole experience was out of body.

I notice the taste has faded, even replaced by a faint sweetness, and my jaw hurts like I've been chewing for days. I look back toward the parking garage before turning the corner. Nobody is chasing me. No woman pointing a finger at me, like "There he is officer . . . the one with the denim jacket."

Once I'm around the corner, I pull the bucket list from my pocket. I've done everything on it. Except for the last entry, which has been scribbled over with a blue pen. Not crossed off as though we'd already done it, but scratched out with an angry hand, nearly ripping through the paper. I can make out a few letters, but that doesn't help. It's illegible. When I finally remember what we'd written, my stomach sinks. It was the most important entry of all. The one we were the most excited about. Something that kept us up nights, something we talked about regularly, dreamt about. But we never crossed it out. Not this one.

I clutch the list in my hand and run home, my nose running, a new taste of copper in my mouth. I'm filled with such shame. Trying to steal a woman's purse at gunpoint? Fucking really? I slow my pace once I'm half a block from home because I see a black sedan parked in front. It's Jerry. No way I'm going home now. I can't deal with him. Not yet. Not like this, my body buzzing with witch dust.

But it's too late. He sees me, and he's bee-lining it, revenge in his eyes. "Get over here, fucker!" he yells.

I'm too tired to run, so I prepare for impact because I know he has no intention on applying the brakes.

Every tooth in my head loosens when his body hits mine. My back meets the pavement, and I cough out any breath I have in me. Before I'm even able to see straight, my cheekbone takes a fist. It doesn't hurt. I'm numb now. Between the witch dust and adrenaline, my nerves are dead. He throws another punch. This one hits the side of my head, and a million school bells ring. I used to love that sound. It used to mean freedom.

"The fuck is this?"

I don't open my eyes, too afraid he's bluffing. He just wants them open to gouge them out.

"What the fuck is this, Brenton? It's in my sister's handwriting."

The note! My eyes fly open. I feel for my back pocket, pull the note out. It's safe. I look at Jerry. He's holding the crumpled bucket list.

"This some kind of to-do list?"

I sit up, scooch away from the street, put my back against a small tree. People on the other side of the street are walking by, half paying attention. What I really want is for a crowd to gather, save me from Jerry's vengeance. "Something like that, yeah."

"What's this last one?"

I lie. "I don't know."

"Is this stuff Rita did?"

I want to tell him no, she never did any of it, I did it. I'm a nice guy. I don't drive people to suicide. I don't steal purses and threaten women. But I lie again. "Yeah, she did."

Jerry's lip quivers. "God bless her." His eyes find mine. They're on fire. "You didn't deserve her."

"I didn't hurt her, Jerry. We were in love. We were gonna get mar—"

"What's that?" He's pointing at the note in my hand. I cradle it close. No way he's getting this.

"What the fuck is that, Brenton?" He pounces, and I cower, then kick. My foot hits his chest but not hard. He grabs my foot and twists it.

I swing blindly and connect with his jaw, ripping the letter in half. Rita's sacred note is open now, like some Egyptian tomb that should have been guarded by curses and plagues, closed forever, and when opened the air fills with blackened swirls of locusts and cancer.

Jerry ignores the punch and goes for the opened tomb, pulling the secret words from the envelope. I'm too shocked to move, too petrified to hold tight the other half, and he snatches it from my sleeping fingers.

"It's all in here, isn't it?" he says, waving the two halves of paper. I recognize the shade of pink. The same pink that covered the pages of a leather-bound journal I'd gotten her, where she'd write poetry, lyrics, memories, observational moments, every one of them meant to make her happy when she felt depressed. The irony lights my gut on fire. "You're fucked now, asshole. It's all coming out."

I watch as Jerry fits the two pieces together and reads. I wait for the fire in his eyes to burn brighter, his hands to tremble, and his knuckles to go white. I want locusts to eat his eyes, the cancer to consume his insides. The letter is mine. It's the most important thing in the world to me. It's my boon and my bane. Private isn't a big enough word. The letter is my sex tape, my diary, and every hidden sin. It's meant for only one set of eyes to flood over, only one heart to break.

His eyes widen, welling up with tears, jaw goes slack. If Jerry won't die from the curse of the tomb, I want him to kill me now, to send me straight to Rita, where I can tell her all about the bucket list and hold her tight, squeezing every last tear from her, every last bit of sadness until she joyfully laughs at the absurdity of my love for her.

"I . . . " Jerry tries to speak but can't. Tears drop, catching on his shirt, darkening it. "I'm . . . really sorry, Brenton. I didn't know." He reaches his hand out to help me up. Behind my anger and fear is a desperation for someone's touch that's much stronger, and I take his hand, then grapple him with a hug. It feels like a reflex I can't control and don't even care to. "I'm so sorry, man," he says. It's a whisper that tells me the letter will kill me if I read it, that it'll be too much to handle.

After a few moments, Jerry pulls away, hands me the letter, then wipes his face on his sleeve, and walks toward his car.

I head down the street to my apartment, while Jerry drives off. I know it's time. I can't fight this forever. I need to face it. Just not here. Not at the apartment I'll never spend another night in. The place we once called home, where we cleaned up and worked hard together to stay that way. But it's tainted now by the memory of blood and of our last embrace in the scarlet tub—her stiff and bluing, me sobbing and frozen, crusted razors nearby where candles once stood. Candles that spotlighted so many nights intertwined—flesh on flesh, tongues dancing, ecstatic howls, and sensual moans. Those memories have been replaced now, like black paint over flowered wallpaper.

CHAPTER 10

I head inside to change my urine-soaked pants. The apartment smells like Rita, accents of body wash, laundry soap, hairspray, and perfume. And I wonder if I'll be one of these people who cling to the idea that ghosts exist and her spirit is always with me, trying to communicate through winning scratch-offs, a perfume-scented breeze, or a bird perched on the windowsill—anything to cope with the loss.

Tough times never last, but tough people do. I wish you would have believed that, baby.

I strip down and change my clothes, look at the bed. I'll never sleep in this room again. I have no plan, only the declaration that me and this apartment are through. I'll couch hop if I have to. I've got friends. They'll understand. I sure as shit ain't gonna sleep in the park. If you can't trust a sweet old lady, who can you trust?

Shit. The gun. The failed holdup. I wish I could make penance for that one, apologize to the woman, let her know that wasn't me. It was a drugged and broken version of me, led by an unstoppable force. Magic? Witchcraft? Psychedelics? It's not even a version of me when I was using. But I have no idea who that poor woman is, and hanging around the parking garage, waiting for her in a dark corner just to apologize, sounds like a bad idea. Whoever she is, she takes no shit. Tough as nails. *Good for her.*

I grab my keys, make sure I have the letter, and head out the door. I take note of every smell along the way, every sight, knowing once I read the letter, my perspective could change, and this right now is the old me. I hope there's some semblance of that person once I'm through.

I breathe in deep once more, then lock up and head to the park.

CHAPTER 11

I'll be honest. After seeing Jerry's reaction to Rita's words, I'm less scared that I'd done something wrong I wasn't aware of, that I was the cause of her ending it. But I know if the letter alluded to something like that even a little bit, Jerry would have finished me there on the sidewalk, regardless of who watched.

With each step I take toward the park, I speculate. I dream of every possible scenario. I guess what I'm trying to do is ponder the worst, so maybe I'll find some relief in the letter, and whatever weight I'm given to carry will feel less burdensome. Was her suicide from guilt? Depression? A sickness she didn't want to suffer through? But every scenario I come up with makes no sense. I knew Rita, everything about her. When she was happy, I knew why. When she was excited, I knew. And most importantly, when she was upset, I knew the cause. It's part of what made us the perfect couple, being fully aware of each other's language. We spoke almost telepathically, reading one another. She had so many tells. Nibbling on the side of her cheek, holding her knees close together and gently rubbing them, running a finger across her earring, the strangest twist upon her lips and twinkle in her eye, a slight change in the tone of her voice, and the wrestling of her toes, rubbing them together. Just a few of the many signs with different meanings. Some meant fear, some arousal, some relief, some anger, some contentment, and some joy. I knew them all. And she knew mine. Body language as subtle as a baby's breath, but ever so loud to us because we knew. We'd studied, we understood, and we catered. But when I needed to hear her most, I couldn't. I'd missed the most important of them all, and I'd give anything to go back and catch it.

Maybe I *am* to blame. That's something I'll probably deal with the rest of my life. Unless this letter—this sacred document—frees me from it.

I see the park in view and feel my sorrow give birth to anger, and then guilt. Guilt because I have the audacity to feel the anger, that I should only feel the grief. But I remember at a meeting once when a woman was talking about losing her sister and the different stages she went through, every one of them an excuse to go back out and start using again. Anger was one of those stages, and for ten minutes she went on about how her sister should have quit drinking, should have been safer, cared more, that she should have loved her own children enough to give a shit what kind of past, present, and future she was offering them. This woman was pissed. And maybe I should be too. Rita left me. She ended us. She deprived us of growing old together, and now I'm alone.

I can just make out the yellow bench up ahead. It's empty. Always is, like it's too ugly for peace of mind. But the fact that nobody ever sat there is exactly why we chose it as our own. We were ugly once, neck deep in needles, but then we cleaned up, and now we have just as much to offer as anyone.

Had. We *had* just as much.

I see an old man teaching a boy how to skip stones across the pond. I see a hooker on the far end of the park near the street, bending over like her ass is a billboard for passersby to reflect on whether or not cheating on their wife is worth it. Many will cave. Every one of them will regret it. I've seen the girl around. She uses but hides it well. Teeth intact, not many sores, not too skinny. Not yet.

I sit on the yellow bench and watch the people around me, doing their own thing, each with their own demons, and I wonder if anyone else is having one of the worst days of their life. Maybe that old man lost someone too. Maybe this park is his sanctuary. Maybe that prostitute on the corner is living her last day on Earth because she can't leave the drugs alone, and the news of her death will spread like a parasite to live inside her siblings and parents and offspring, wishing they could have done something more for her, going through the phases, a few of them holding tight to anger because the woman didn't try harder.

I pull the pieces of letter from my pocket. This is the moment. It's like God is trusting me with the meaning of life and the potential regret I'll feel for wasting so many years chasing a high, then more years waking up.

I stall. My hands are sweaty, shaky. It's surreal. Unreal. Like just before I read that first word, I'll wake up, and Rita will be there in my arms, between the sheets, with her hair tickling my face. And I'll thank the good Lord it was all a bad dream and live the rest of my life with the most sincere sense of gratitude, never taking anything for granted.

But there is no waking up. This is life now. Me, the letter, the park bench, and whatever comes next.

I hold the two pieces of the letter together and stare at the first two words: *"Dearest Brenton."*

I read the words countless times while the rest teases my peripheral. I speak the words out loud, making them real, feeling the bittersweet on my tongue, the devastation through my ears.

"Dearest Brenton."

I hold my breath and go on.

I'm sorry. I'm sorry for today, for tomorrow, for ten years from now, for every scar this will cause. And I pray you'll somehow understand.

My eyes are drowning, and I can't see anything but the blurring ink written under black duress. I blink, forcing the tears to fall. The page wet, and the ink runs like mascara.

I was never going to tell you why. I wanted to take every bit of it with me to the grave. Not a soul would ever know what could have been . . . what should have been. But you deserve to know.

Do you remember our list?

I want so badly to shout with laughter at the irony and share with her what I've been doing the past two days and the crazy adventure it was.

Do you remember our last entry?

I do. And the thought of it never being able to happen kills me.

It almost happened, my love. I carried our child for weeks, growing, preparing to meet the two people who would do everything they could to make it feel loved, to protect it. But the day I found out, before I could leap into your arms and share with you the miracle, it spilled out of me.

A guttural scream escapes me, and I don't even realize I've made the nightmarish sound until people through the park stop what they're doing and turn to me—pieces of pink paper crumpled in my trembling hands.

Out of all the scenarios I considered, this was never one of them. My heart splits in two, and my mind cracks at the thought of losing not only my lover but our creation. I know exactly how the rest of the letter will read.

I hold the letter up once more and skim through the lines, looking for keywords. They're all there. Guilt regarding her past and the damage she'd done to her body, taking blame for the loss of our child due to her choices, that she robbed us of our dream, of the most important thing on our list—an entry so important it didn't belong on the same page as pissing on a cop's car or stealing from the rich to give to the poor, or helping the homeless. This entry deserved its own place. It wasn't some novelty or a moment of self-satisfaction. This was us performing a miracle and giving it every bit of love we could muster.

I watch the old man turn from the pond, an unlit clove cigarette in his mouth. His face looks like mine, full of weight from too much grief. I recognize the eyes that could care less if they ever saw anything again, the mouth that just as soon be stitched shut, and I hope for his sake, and for mine, that his grief is new and not decades old, that there would be some semblance of moving on and healing. I need to know this is a fresh wound and not some old scar, like an old pair of soleless shoes he tolerates with each step, every waking moment.

I run to him. "Sir . . . Sir, is there healing after this?"

He looks me over, sees the paper in my hands, the red in my glassy eyes. "I'm not sure yet." His voice holds so much sorrow, so much uncertainty. "But I'm working on it." Then he puffs on his unlit smoke and walks away.

I head back to the bench and read the letter in full. Twice. I speak to Rita as though she's God, listening to my every word. I tell her it's not her fault, that she deserved life and deserved to try again and again and not give up, that heroin isn't what took our dream. My words become a babbling mantra periodically interrupted by running phlegm and dry heaves.

I can think of nowhere else to go and nothing else to do, so I spend the rest of the day and night on the yellow park bench, reciting the letter, speaking truths aloud to every lie she must have believed.

CHAPTER 12

I spend the next two weeks couch hopping between friends and going to the park, looking for the old man. He's the only person I feel I can relate to, despite not knowing a thing about him. I wait for him because I need to know things will get better, to know he's figured shit out, that moving on is a possibility. But I never see him again. To get me through and my mind on track, I tell myself he hasn't come back because figuring shit out is exactly what he did, and now he doesn't need the peace of mind a long gaze at the pond can offer. He's moved on.

Finally, I give up. On everything. Going to the park, holding out hope, and staying sober, which felt inevitable since the moment I found Rita in the tub, like holding onto sobriety was a lie, and eventually I'd embrace the needle once again. A road to destruction paved by the jagged slice of a razorblade, and here I am, cash in hand, walking down the boulevard to an old hot spot I used to score at. From there, I'll head to a park to boot up. I certainly can't do it at my friend's place.

"Good to see you again, B," the dealer says. I want to knock his teeth out, him reveling in my return. Fucker.

I can feel the old lies with the same voices, telling me this is a one-time thing and that this time I won't let it get out of control. It's all bullshit, and I know it. But I humor the voice and listen anyway.

I find a group of bushes in the park that's prime real estate for nodding off. It's a sandbox of paraphernalia. Used needles, broken, bent, and rusty. Empty bottles, empty lighters, and small baggies that have probably been licked clean and tapped for every miniscule grain.

I dig in the dirt with my hands and bury my wallet, cover it with leaves. There's no lock on this door of evergreen foliage, so chances on waking up with empty pockets is pretty good.

I prep, then stare at the needle. Liquid gold Rita and I used to call it, then when we cleaned up, we called it fool's gold. Part of me wants the batch to be spiked, a dash of fentanyl to take me out of the misery. No, not part of me. Every bit of me wants that.

I roll up my sleeve and tie off, the needle clenched in my teeth. Then I hear a distant voice, a familiar one I can't place. I pull my feet to my ass, make sure they're not sticking out, make sure I can't be seen. The voice is female, growing closer. It's not someone I know well, maybe from a meeting. I'm running every feminine face I see at the tables through my head and coming up empty. But when the voice is nearly on top of me, and a ratty old tennis shoe appears where I'd crawled into the tiny, green cubby hole, I realize it's that crazy bitch with the powder.

"I saw you go in there, young man," she says. All I can see is her feet.

I'm like a child hiding from his mother, knowing damn well I'm not fooling her.

"What do you want, old lady?"

"I came to apologize. I shouldn't have sent you on that ride. I thought maybe you were ready. But you can't go on a quest like that with a head full of what I suspect was anger buried in that grief, maybe guilt too."

I don't say anything and wait for her to leave.

"What are you doing in there, anyway?"

"I'm minding my own business, that's what I'm doing."

"Did you read the letter? Is that why you're in there? Hiding from the world now?"

"Ma'am . . . I'm just trying to be alone, so would you please—"

She brings her voice down like she's not even talking to me anymore but someone else. "He's in there doing drugs, tryin' to ruin his life. What do I do?"

And here we go again with the voices.

"Get out of there, young man. Don't be stupid."

I feel like an idiot, couldn't feel any more like one. Legs tucked under me, hiding in the bushes, arguing with an old woman about my life choices.

"I'm not interested in your help, lady. Now, go talk to your invisible friends and leave me alone."

"Fine," she says, then I see her feet move, turning back where she came from. "But you're making a big mistake, and you know it. You could be kickin' life in the balls like it did you. But you're gonna wallow the rest of your days." She mumbles something to the voices again I can't make out, then, "Tough days don't last, but tough people do."

The needle falls from my mouth, lands in the dirt. I let go of the tie and replay the last thing she said, over and over again, letting it linger like a continuous echo. I look down at the needle and shudder at how close I came to giving up. This isn't what Rita wanted. She wanted to be free of guilt, free from the idea that she ruined someone else's life. If she knew I was heading down that path on account of her, she'd kill herself all over again.

I stomp the needle with the heel of my foot until it breaks, and fool's gold pours out. I grab my wallet from the shallow hole climb out from the bushes.

The woman is walking away, carrying a canvas bag in one hand, and a paperback book in the other. I catch up to her, put my hand on her shoulder.

"Say it again," I tell her.

"Say what again? About tough people?"

"Yeah. Say it again . . . please."

"I can't remember how it goes." She turns her head, like she's listening to someone else, then back to me. With the strangest twist upon her lips, she says, "Tough days don't last, but tough people do."

"Where'd you hear that?"

She smiles and says, "I'm just a crazy old lady, dear." Then walks away.

I stand there dumbfounded, wanting to believe that Rita spoke through her, offering the same words I'd preached to her so many times. And I realize in that moment that I've just joined those who believe in mysterious signs of loved ones looking after like angels, sending ominous messages by way of oddly-shaped clouds, perfume-scented breezes, and birds on the windowsill. And I wonder if maybe it's not just about coping. Maybe it's about believing.

My Only Sunshine

Robert Ford

FOR THE SAKE of simplicity, I'll round it off to four months and three days, but I know—down to the minute— exactly how long it's been since they found my daughter's body. It's not something I have to focus on. I do it without thinking, like breathing.

It's part of who I am now.

My alarm goes off at 5:15 and I sit up immediately. I've learned it's best to get moving and avoid falling back into the lull of a warm, but lonely, bed. Getting up right away also helps me not think about the mornings she would crawl in beside me with her teddy bear, Bobo, clutched tightly in her arms. We'd lay there and whisper, even though there was no real reason to be quiet. I don't want to think about those mornings because I miss them so much. I miss snuggling and making each other giggle in the early light.

It takes me thirty-six minutes to shower, dress, put on make-up, and walk fourteen steps downstairs to the first floor.

Brewing a half-pot of coffee takes four minutes and twenty-three seconds right down to the last drip. Another twenty-one minutes to eat a yogurt—plain vanilla or blackberry, if you're interested—finish my second cup of coffee, catch the morning news, hit the bathroom, and then I'm out the door and on my way to the office.

The traffic to Harrisburg varies, but on average, it's nineteen minutes from my front door to the parking garage. Nine minutes to get from the parking garage to the front lobby of the office building where I work, and that includes a stop at the street cart vendor to grab a large coffee. The stuff they brew at the office is borderline criminal and, besides that, I like to support local businesses.

From the office building lobby, I check the two elevators and see which floor is lit up. If there's an elevator on the ground floor, I waltz right in—no time for hesitation. I work on the eleventh floor, so based on an average of three to five people in the elevator, even if they all stop on separate floors—which never happens—and considering two or three stops, average about twelve seconds of doors opening and closing again, I arrive at the eleventh floor in approximately three minutes, forty-three seconds from the lobby.

From the elevator, it takes me sixty-eight steps to reach my desk. A minute and a half to remove my jacket, take a healthy drink of my coffee, and get settled at my desk.

That is a *normal* morning for me. I have become the white rabbit from *Alice in Wonderland*, always with a pocket watch in one hand and a schedule to keep.

I wasn't always like this.

This morning is *not* normal.

I pull into the parking garage at Walnut and Second Street and find a spot on the fourth floor. I never take the elevator because it's old and shaky, and though I *can* imagine getting stuck inside with its urine stink and graffitied stainless-steel interior, I won't allow myself the chance to do so.

I approach the stairwell. The split-second before I touch the door handle, it swings wide open, and the man standing there freezes in place, stares at me like . . . no, not stares, he *studies* me. I hesitate a moment, waiting for him to step out onto the floor, and in that brief instant, he pulls a short-barreled revolver from his filthy jean jacket.

"Gimme your fuckin' purse, bitch."

His voice is full of road gravel and I wonder if it's from an injury or from years of nicotine abuse. I decide it doesn't matter, and tighten my grip on my purse. His eyes widen, and he cocks his head slightly.

"I said, gimme your fuckin' purse!"

The barrel of the revolver is a black hole, and I'm not naïve to the deathly treasure on the other side of that dark pit. I look up from the revolver and meet in his eyes.

"No."

His face pinches. "Fuck you say to me? Bitch, I will put a goddamn bullet in—"

"Then do it."

The man's face twists up even more, and his expression is an odd oil slick on water mixture of pain and uncertainty. He stiffens his arm, holds the pistol out straight, and aims it at my face.

"Lady, I will fuck you up if—"

"You're not getting my purse, so either pull the trigger or don't pull the trigger, but quit wasting my time." I realize my heart is not racing. Adrenaline is not flooding through my veins, kicking in the fight or flight instinct, and even though that should worry me, it doesn't.

The man doesn't seem to know what to do. He reaches his other hand up and scratches his head through his knit stocking hat. He snaps his free hand out to grab at my purse strap, but   I easily turn away to avoid him.

"I said *no*." I'm a bit surprised at the tone of my voice. It's calm, but stern, the voice of an elementary school teacher scolding an unruly child.

"You crazy ass Bitch, I will fucking—"

"Then fucking do it!" I scream, and my voice is no longer calm. I step closer, lean my forehead against the cool circle of the barrel. The sensation is somehow soothing, and I have a sudden flashback to a night in college, drunk and throwing up, being oddly comforted by the cold touch of a porcelain toilet.

He jerks his hand away and suddenly turns back toward the stairwell, but the pocket of his jacket gets caught on the handle of the door. He spins sideways and the gun falls to the cement landing as he stumbles down several steps and slams against the wall.

I reach down and pick up his revolver. It's heavier than I thought it would be, and though the steel is shiny, it's covered with fingerprint smudges. The rubber grip is sticky against the palm of my hand.

"Hey, hey now . . . yo lady, look . . . " His voice has lost even a hint of aggression. It holds the calm, soothing tone of a therapist, a hostage negotiator. He's standing with his back against the wall, holding his hands out toward me in the universally recognized calm down gesture.

There's no need. I'm calm again. I raise the pistol in his direction and beneath his grimy, whiskered face, I actually watch the color drain out. His Adam's apple works as he swallows hard, and then he lunges away from the wall and down the stairwell. I hear him jumping down the short flights, his hand squeaking along the steel railings, and then the metallic punch as he slams the first-floor door open.

I close my eyes and inhale deeply. This is not to calm myself. This idiot made me late, and I hate being late. I stuff the revolver into my purse and hear my footsteps echo as I walk downstairs.

—◆—

I settle into my cubicle and log into my computer. I know from experience, it'll be approximately twenty seconds before Ivan pops his head over the cubicle wall, like a groundhog with a Pavlovian response to my PC's start-up chime.

"Good morning, Caroline."

Ivan has been in the country for over twenty years, but he still has a thick Russian accent. Last year at the company Christmas party was the first time I have ever seen Ivan drunk, and by the time his wife ushered him away, Ivan sounded like Boris from *Rocky and Bullwinkle*. He's nice enough as a cubicle neighbor, and I could've done a lot worse.

"Hello and good morning to you, Ivan. How's your day going so far?"

"It's good, good." He glances away from me in the direction of our boss's office, before his gaze returns to me. "Scott was looking for you earlier. He said he wants to see you."

I lean sideways on my chair, far enough to peek around my cubicle wall. Through the partially closed window blinds of Scott's office, I see him standing and moving around his desk.

"He say what for?"

Ivan shakes his balding head. "Just to tell you when you got in. Late this morning? You okay?"

I straighten in my seat and take a drink of coffee. Since I was running late anyway, I decided to not break routine, and stop at the street vendor. Enough of my schedule had been screwed up this morning, and there is no way I could handle the black tar in the office coffee pot.

"Yeah, I'm okay, I just uh . . . ran into an old friend before I got here is all."

I stand, take my coffee with me, and head toward Scott's office. I knock twice on his heavy, wooden door and hear him tell me to come in.

Scott is standing, hands on his hips, chair pushed to the side, and staring at organized piles on his desk. I am struck at how much he resembles Mark Twain with a slightly less wild mustache. I wonder if he has ever dressed up as Twain for Halloween, but decide it's best to not ask.

Scott glances up at me and offers a small but brief hint of a smile before he turns his attention to his desk again. "Ever play Magic the Gathering?"

"I . . . don't think so, no."

"My son got introduced to it at camp last summer and sucked me into it. The little shit has kicked my ass the last six times we played and I've had it. Building my own deck of Angels to kick his Eldrazi's ass."

I have absolutely no idea what to say as a response to this, and so I stand there quietly and take another sip of my coffee as Scott continues to study his various stacks of cards. He takes a deep breath, shakes his head, and clears his throat.

"I'll deal with this later. Do me a favor and close the door."

I've always been a good employee, so there's no reason for me to think I'm in trouble or have done anything wrong, but five months ago, Scott's words would have made my stomach curl into knots of wet rope and send anxiety flooding through my veins. Right now, it does nothing at all, and I close the door, hearing the heavy *thunk* as it shuts.

"Have a seat, please."

I sit down in one of the plush leather chairs in front of Scott's desk. He has already settled into his chair, and he leans forward, elbows on his desk. "Caroline, you doing okay?"

I realize it's the second time this morning I've been asked this question, but I auto-respond with a nod of my head. "Yeah, I'm good, Scott. I am. Why do you ask?"

He exhales slowly and opens a manila folder to the side of the card stacks. There's several papers inside and he scans the information. "You're doing a good job, Caroline. You are, and I don't want you to think you're underappreciated." He flips the folder closed again and leans back in his chair. "You've always done a good job."

"Okay, so then what—"

"Your call rate has flatlined for the last two months. Look . . . " He leans forward, elbows on the desk again. "There's nothing wrong with that, okay? You're not doing badly, but you're not doing well . . . except, you are. It's like you stopped reaching, and it's understandable you know, not pushing yourself after . . . " He glances down as everyone always does when they discuss something even remotely close to what happened, to what I've been through. "You've had a lot to deal with, and I wanted to check in and make sure you're happy here."

I drink from my foam cup of coffee and give another automatic nod. The truthful answer is I'm really not sure if I am happy here, but I do know I'm not unhappy, which seems to be the correct thing to focus on. "Yeah, Scott, I'm . . . I'm good. Really."

His gaze hangs on me a moment, and then he reopens the folder, shifts some papers inside, and pulls one free. Scott looks it over and then puts it on the desk in front of me. It's a calendar of the next three months.

"I want you to take a look over the next quarter and figure out a time to take a week's vacation. You don't have to tell me today, but soon. It's mandatory."

"What? Scott, I'm—"

"It's not me." He holds his hand up to cut me off. "Cindy in HR went to some seminar on workplace violence . . . people who don't take enough vacation to de-stress do bad shit in the office or something. You know how it is. Some guy snaps and brings in a loaded—"

"Is that what you think I'm gonna do? Come in and shoot up the place?"

Scott's face pinches up like he bit into a lemon wedge and he shakes his head. "No, no, I don't think that. It's . . . wait, you don't *own* a gun, do you?"

"Scott!" I know my expression has to be incredulous, and he lets an amused smirk replace the pained look on his face.

"Of course, I don't think you're going to do anything like that. Not at all." He releases a heavy sigh. "Caroline, you've been served up cold shit on a hot plate this year. We both know that. But don't whine about this. You have two weeks of vacation accrued, and if you don't use a week before the end of the year, you'll lose it anyway."

I exhale, maybe a bit too heavily, and Scott notices.

"Look, you're not alone. Cindy's making Brad in Accounting take a few days off, too."

"Oh, God. What happened to Brad?"

"His turtle died last week."

"His—"

"Turtle, yeah. Wasn't like Brad was crying at his desk or anything. I think he already got another one, some Japanese redsnouted . . . something or other, I don't freakin' know." Scott shakes his head. "Point is, don't feel singled out."

Scott smiles and his voice softens to a low considerate tone. "Go to a beach or something. Hell, stay in your pajamas all day, eat ice cream, and binge-watch something if you want, but friend to friend, Caroline, take the fuckin' vacation."

I stare into Scott's eyes and I see the kindness there. He's always been a fair boss, but more than that, he's one of the rare breeds that actually seems to care about his employees. I nod at him and offer a slight smile.

"Okay, okay. I'll think about the dates and let you know. I'll take a week next month."

"All right, good." Scott pats his hand once on the desk and nods approval. "Now go on, get back to it. And hey? When you're making calls today, reach a little bit, okay?"

"You got it."

I swing open Scott's heavy office door and return it to the barely open position I found it in earlier. Ivan is chattering away on his phone as I return to my cubicle. I sit down, take another drink of my still-warm coffee and position it on my desk as far away from the computer as possible. As I roll my chair into place, my left foot bumps against my purse beneath my desk, and I stare at the dull rubber grip on the revolver tucked inside.

∽

The office is a stereotype of what an office should be. It's the kind of place set designers would visit before creating interiors for a sitcom. Plants polka-dot the landscape—some fake, some real but living on borrowed time. My own contributions to the indoor forest are two tiny air plants and a cactus on my shelf. The air plants you almost have to do something intentional like drench them with gasoline and set them on fire to kill them. They literally live off air. My cactus is a small but plump spiky button that blooms the most beautiful magenta flower, but it seems to make up its own routine instead of adhering to any pre-determined schedule from nature itself.

I used to have a sweet potato vine that sat on top of my cubicle and reached the floor, but one night it apparently got caught in the vacuum of someone on the cleaning crew and brought the entire thing crashing to the carpet. Didn't think plants could experience trauma like people do, but I watered it and gave it plant food, even played Mozart and talked to the damned thing every morning. It withered up and turned brown within a week and that was the end of that.

Someone is softly playing easy listening music, and if I strain to listen, I can hear someone else with talk radio blabbering on about politics. The sounds of the office are mostly contained behind the cubicle walls and tan, metal shelving holding startlingly similar rows of white and black binders.

Obligatory family photos are displayed on a shelf here, a desk corner there. Some stickers or Post-it notes or newspaper comics taped to the edge of computer monitors. Anything unique but not intrusive, so employees can claim the seven by five space as theirs.

Beside the plants in my cubicle, the only other decoration I currently have is a single sticky note hanging from the bottom of my monitor. It has a small and crude drawing, in thick red marker, of a ribbon—not the kind you wear to raise money for a cause, but the kind you get for winning a contest. To the right of the ribbon, as equally crude, are distorted and out of proportion words written in an unsteady hand: BEST MOMMY EVER!!

I stare at the note longer than I should and then force myself to turn toward my computer monitor and get to work.

～

It's just before noon and I'm hungry. That feels unusual because most days I eat because I should, because I have to . . . because if I don't, I'll actually forget. I'll get sick and wither away as helplessly as my dead sweet potato vine.

But like I said, today is not a normal day.

I reach inside the cabinet and pull out a package of microwaveable noodles and head toward the office kitchen. I'm alone and get the pleasure of not having to wait for Simone in Accounting to microwave some disgusting leftover fish dish from the night before, or Eaton in Marketing to over-nuke his popcorn and leave the slight charcoal smell behind him.

I lean against the sink as my noodles heat up. There's new flyers posted to the bulletin board, and I read part of an HR Announcement about proper dress attire in the workplace, even though there is no one, literally no one in this office who would push boundaries of good taste when it comes to clothing. I read the top two paragraphs and skip to the bottom, look at the illustrations of acceptable skirt length, and proper depth of blouse collar.

"Something smells good in here."

I turn to the voice and see Mimi, the mail-lady, standing at the doorway. We exchange quick smiles. Mimi is a kind-hearted soul, as some people say. She has worked here since before I started, and that was over eleven years ago. Every day, Mimi delivers the inner-office mail with a smile on her face. If anyone is having a rough day, Mimi's there, even if for a brief moment, to lift your spirits and make you laugh. Sometimes, if she's not too loaded down, she'll pause long enough to fold origami out of sticky notes. A little swan or frog, sometimes a cat or a hummingbird. I have a bright pink crane sitting in the paperclip tray on my desk.

"You want some, Mimi? I'll share!"

"*Nooooo, no.* You go on and eat your lunch. You need it more than me." Her smile grows wider and Mimi shakes her head. She glances behind her and then takes a step into the kitchen. When she speaks, it's in a low voice. "How are you, Miss Caroline?"

"I'm okay, Mimi. There's . . . good and bad days, but it's been a while since I've had a bad day, you know?"

After everything happened, Mimi is one of the few people who checked on me for a few weeks after. She also brought over a homemade dish of the best Vietnamese food I've ever had.

She reaches out and takes my hands in hers. I realize it's been months since I've touched another person at all, let alone held their hands. This should bring me comfort, but it only makes me want to yank my hands away and stuff them in my pockets. I know Mimi means well, so I don't.

"*Mmmm.* Miss Caroline . . . " She gives a slight, disapproving shake of her head. "I can see it in your eyes. That hollow there. The hurt. I know." Mimi gives my hands a slight squeeze and then lets them go.

I'm not sure I disagree with her, so I don't know how to respond to her observation. Thankfully, the microwave *dings* and I open the door and withdraw my steaming noodles. The container is hotter than I expect, so I put it down on the counter. Steam curls up and away from it.

"Take this. It'll help."

I turn to Mimi and look down at the business card she holds out.

"No, Mimi. I don't need a grief counselor or—"

"It's not that, Miss Caroline. But there's a cost." Mimi checks behind her again, and then turns back to me. Her voice lowers to a whisper. "Best four hundred dollars I ever spent."

She holds the card out toward me and I hesitate a moment, then take it from her hands. "You've done this, Mimi?"

"When my husband passed away, we were young . . . *ohhhh, so young*. We'd been married for only five years when he died. I didn't know how I could go on living. I didn't care anymore, about anything at all really, but especially myself."

Mimi fidgets with the seam of her blouse, touches her fingertips to the buttons. She let out a heavy sigh and continued. "Friend of mine gave me that card. It helped the only way anything *could* help, and I hope it helps you, too."

I open my mouth to speak, but no actual words come to mind, so I simply nod at Mimi and put the card in my pants pocket. The old woman smiles and returns to pushing her mail cart along the row of cubicles, and I turn back to my noodles. The heat has toned down a bit, and now, instead of appearing like a steam grate, the package looks like it has a tiny ghost hovering above it.

⁓⁓⁓

I know I seem like the type of person to have a cat or two, but I don't. It's not that I dislike them, but I grew up without any real sort of pet besides a brown and white hamster that died from wet tail a month after I got it. Emma always wanted a kitten, asked to get one at least twice a month, but it never seemed like the right . . .

It just never . . .

Anyway, I pull into my driveway and see the next-door neighbor, Darren, standing by his front door. He waves and I give a brief wave back. Except for Sundays, Darren is almost always at home. Handsome enough, I guess, in a fit family-sitcom dad sort of way, but talking with him . . . it's like wearing a wool sweater. It's warm and friendly enough, but it's irritating even when it's not really irritating if that makes sense.

Conversations with Darren are boring, and I truly cannot stand banality anymore. I cannot deal with the filler content people use in between the real stuff. I suppose I've stripped myself down, along with my patience, to the kind of things that actually matter.

Raindrops patter down on my windshield, and I'm thankful. I'm positive if it weren't raining, Darren would walk over to say hello in person, and I cannot deal with his triteness today.

I park my car and get out quickly, yelling a "*Oooh*, it's starting to rain!" toward Darren, who is now at the bottom step of his front porch, because, sure as shit, he was heading in my direction. I ignore him as I dash for my house, and twenty-three footsteps later, I stand there, open the front door, and charge inside.

Right as I set my purse down, my phone rings. I pull it free and press the *Answer* button without even checking the number. "Hello?"

"Hey, uh . . . it's me."

Even the sound of his voice doesn't turn my stomach like it used to. Does that mean I'm healed or am I still healing? I think about this question and choose to not respond.

"Hello? Caroline?"

I sigh and stare toward the kitchen. "I'm here."

"Just wanted to make sure you're okay."

I pull the phone away from my ear and stare at it, wondering how I can send my expression through the cell signal so he can see my disgust.

"Alan, you don't have to pay child support anymore, okay? You have a little more pocket money every—"

"Oh, fuck you, Caroline."

"Fuck *me?* No, Alan, fuck—"

"I'm calling because I wanted to—"

"Alan, you left Emma long before she was dead, so there's no real reason to call me again. Ever. She was the only thing tying us together, and that was a thin thread at best."

I hear soft rustling on the other end of the call, and then a breathy sob from Alan. "Goddamn you, she was my daughter, too, Caroline, I—"

I pull the phone away from my ear and end the call, lay it on the table in the foyer, and then cross the living room with a practiced gait. There are photos in the living room, various pictures framed in everything from weathered barn wood to bubblegum pink plastic in the shape of one of those waving cats on the counters of Asian restaurants.

Almost every single one of the photographs has Emma in it, and I'm not ready to look at them all. Because I know that'll happen if my gaze pauses on even one of the pictures. I'll have to look at each and every one of them, remembering what was going on when the photo was taken, reliving that moment when Emma was alive.

I'll see how cute she was, and then I won't be able to not think of how she looked when they found her, bone white and bloody.

No, I'm not ready yet.

My well-honed walk takes me through the living room and up the stairs, where I take a right turn into my bedroom.

I kick my shoes into my closet and take off my work clothes. I toss the blouse into my dirty-clothes basket, and then hold my black slacks at arm's length by the waist. I fold them and grab a plastic hanger from my closet, and that's when I see it laying on the floor—the business card Mimi gave me earlier.

It's an unusual card, at least information wise. There's no phone number, email, or website, nothing but the address of 1443 Pearl Street, and a small yellow crown above the type.

I sit on my bed, dressed only in my bra and panties, and stare at the business card. After a moment, I feel hot tears rolling down my cheeks before I realize I'm crying. I know there is something wrong with me, but at the same time, I think, under the circumstances, maybe it's normal to feel this way . . . to not feel as a feeling. I take a deep, slow inhale, hold my breath and close my eyes, and then just as slowly, exhale until my head feels floaty behind my eyelids.

I look at the card again and lay it on the bed.

I feel like a jackass as I pull on a pair of jeans and my sage green sweater.

I feel like an absolute idiot as I walk downstairs with Bobo in my hands, sit the Teddy bear up on the couch toward the TV.

And for the love of all that's holy, I feel like a complete and utter moron when I start my car and pull out of my driveway.

But here I am, hitting up an ATM for four hundred dollars for something . . . I don't even know what it is, let alone if it'll help me or not. I fold the cash in half and stuff it into a front pocket of my purse.

Passing through the center of downtown, it's a general rule to avoid any street named after precious gems or stones. Three blocks outside of center square, Diamond, Ruby, and Emerald are absolute hell holes of prostitutes, drug deals, and all-around bad news.

Beyond Emerald are four more streets named after famous musicians, and though I've often wondered, I have never done any research on how this came to be. Those blocks, Beethoven, Fitzgerald, Joplin, and Morrison, have become some sort of an odd barrier against the criminal element, almost as if the names themselves command some sort of respectful behavior. New age shops, art galleries, indie record stores, and a few adult shops mark those blocks, along with microbreweries and coffee bistros.

Before now, I've never gone to the arts district or beyond. I've never had any reason.

I nonchalantly push the door-lock button in my car, as if someone is watching and will be offended by the accusatory act of me locking my doors. When I pass Emerald Street, the relief is almost immediate. I have gone through the wasteland and made it through intact, and I let out a breath I didn't realize I'd been holding. People smile and laugh as they walk along the sidewalks. I hear music spilling from some open-air bars. The buildings in the so-called arts district are vibrantly painted and well taken care of.

I stop at Morrison Street, and ahead of me, I see the blinking yellow light a block ahead. The destination dot on my phone screen shows me I'm not far away, which is good, because I'm not a fan of how quickly things are degrading again. The sidewalks are bookended by dead stores with sun-faded plywood boarding up their windows. There are absolutely no open shops, not even so much as a corner convenience store or a pawn shop. There is zero traffic on the street, as well as the sidewalk, and even the street lamps are an uneven balance of light and dark, like an old hag's smile.

As I approach Chestnut Street, I slow down and glance in my rearview mirror. Not a single pair of headlights in the street behind me. This part of the city is an amputated appendage that doesn't realize it's nothing but dead flesh.

I make a right turn and pull my car to a stop along the darkened sidewalk. According to my GPS, the address is on my left and I see an ornate, protruding entrance to what appears to be an old theatre marquee, complete with baroque curlicues and fleur-de-lis decorating the side panels.

One of the columns supporting the marquee displays the

address numbers, spray painted vertically on the bricks, and the rest of the deep-set entrance is cloaked in shadow except for one tiny thing—a bright yellow light the size of a man's fist, in the shape of a king's crown.

"What the hell am I doing here?"

According to my address, I've arrived, but my mind also believes this would be a great place to get mugged, raped, or stabbed. Trash is piled up along the sides of the entrance, including a half-burned green couch and a stack of wooden pallets.

"Fuck this." I shift my car back into DRIVE but my foot remains on the brake pedal. I grit my teeth and think of Mimi handing the card to me, the concerned expression of sympathy on her face. It makes me wonder how long it will be before I'm ready to look at the photos in the living room. How long before I realize I'm allowed to let myself cry instead of pushing everything down so deep that my body takes over and spills tears on its own while my brain tries to catch up.

I chew my bottom lip and check the rearview mirror and there's nothing—not even a rat crossing the street. Ahead of me and to the sides, it is the same gray landscape, void of motion and vibrancy and any notion at all of life.

"*Fucccckkkkkkk.*" I draw out my whisper, throw the car back into PARK, and kill the engine. My eyes adjust to the dim light and as I approach the front of the building, I see a set of wide, brass-handled doors. In its heyday, this place must have been glorious. I reach for one of the door-handles and let out a whipped-dog yelp as it opens quickly toward me.

A young woman stands behind the gap of the partially opened door. A thin and delicate diamond tiara rests on her head, balancing attention between it and her face, a Beyoncé lookalike, a face which could have been clipped from the cover of any beauty magazine on the newsstands. Around her thin, graceful neck, she wears a matching diamond collar, and from it are at least a dozen tendrils of diamond strings, trailing down over her bare breasts.

"Oh, I . . . " I take a step back from the door. "I think maybe I'm at the wrong—"

"You came to the right place." Her accent is heavily Jamaican. "Come in, come in."

I study her eyes—bright and clear and most importantly, sober—and find them and her smile sincere. Behind the girl, I can see the glow of yellow light. I take a step forward, and then another, and I'm inside, listening to the heavy *ca-chunk* of the door closing.

"This way, please."

The girl leads me down a hallway with an arched ceiling, painted a vibrant, deep purple. Her hips sway hypnotically in the shape of an infinity sign. She wears a diamond belly chain and nothing else below. I look at her smooth, bare skin for a moment longer, and then the hallway opens up into an enormous high-ceilinged space—my assumption is the theatre itself, though any seats that may have been here in the past are long gone to make way for what exists here now.

Everything around me, every single thing is the same sunshine yellow. Even the overhead lights stream a buttercup glow, almost eliminating any shadows.

Plaster friezes decorate the walls, depictions of men in horse-drawn chariots wearing armor and mohawk-topped helmets. The ceiling is arched and divided into diamond shapes by ornate moldings and decorative millwork.

Everything is the same lemon-yellow tone. The only contrast in the room are the girls—easily fifty of them—all in a state of undress like my escort, and spread across several long rows of chaise lounge chairs. Women of every shade of skin and hair color, some of them laying down and arching their backs away from the cushioned seat, others sitting, legs spread wide, hands resting on their knees.

"Please."

I have stopped without realizing it, and I glance ahead to my guide, who is smiling and waving me on. I start walking and look ahead to where the girl is leading me.

At the front of the theatre is the stage, and in the middle of the stage is a purple throne at least a house-story high and the width of a taxi. The man who sits there uncrosses his legs and leans forward, elbows on his knees. Long dreadlocks tumble from his shoulders and I see they almost reach his feet. He wears a three-piece suit, shirt and necktie beneath, a felt fedora, and shoes polished to a fine sheen. All in yellow, including the pair of sunglasses he wears, shining all the more brightly against his skin, the color of roasted coffee beans.

I stumble going up the four steps to get to the stage, and the girl turns around, reaching to steady me, but I wave her off. She walks to within a few feet of the throne, gives a small bow to the man, and walks off stage behind a massive, flowing yellow curtain.

"Yeah, I don't uh . . . I don't think I'm . . . "

The man grins and then chuckles lightly. When he speaks, his voice carries the same patois as the young woman. "You in the right place. I can smell the grief on you, comin' off in waves . . . I can breathe it in like burned chicory root, bitter and raw."

His nostrils flare for a moment, and then he straightens, leans back in his chair. He takes his hat off and places it on his right knee.

"Yeah, uh . . . I just wanted to—"

"I *know* what you want. You want what all the others want, a closure, an endin' of some kind . . . an endin' to your pain, so you can *feeeeel* somethin' else again. All of you the same, but none of you livin' anymore. You all as dead as the ones you grieve." He turns his head slightly and motions with two fingers.

"I already know what you want, but I can't offer that. I can only provide the means to an end . . . what you do with it is up to you."

The young woman from earlier walks to the throne, gives a small cloth bag to the man, and disappears beyond the curtain again. He loosens the drawstring and shakes the contents into the palm of his hand. He hides whatever it is in his fist and holds it up to me. "This is up to fate. Ain't no way 'round it, y' hear?"

I stare at his closed hand and nod, put my hand beneath his, and feel the contents drop against my skin. It's a pair of dice, bright yellow with purple dots.

The man waves his hand to the floor in front of his polished shoes, and I shake the dice in the palm of my hand once, twice, and then let them fall to the wooden stage. One bounces and flips over to three purple dots. The other die does a slow spin on one point and then lands to show a two.

A soft grunt escapes the man. He purses his lips and gives a nod. "Once more."

I lean down, retrieve the dice and toss them again, ending up with a one and a four.

"For the next five nights, including tonight . . . be here before midnight . . . " He reaches inside his suit and pulls out a scrap of paper, hands it to me, and I see there's an address written on it. He points to the dice by his feet. "Fourteen minutes per night."

"I . . . I don't understand what that mea—"

"You will." He scoops the dice from the floor, drops them into the cloth sack in his hand, and leans back with a sigh. "You brought my fee?"

"Yes, of course, I . . . " I withdraw the folded cash from my purse and put it in his outstretched palm. "I'm not sure what I'm paying for . . . what does this—"

"When the time is over, return this to me." He holds a single brass key in front of him, pinched between his index finger and thumb like it's something dirty. "Don't make me come fetch it. That would be . . . unpleasant."

I take the key from him and it feels heavier than it should as I put it in my pocket.

"You have five visits of fourteen minutes. That's it, and that's all. How you spend that time is up to you."

I start to ask a question but I'm not even sure what to ask, so I nod understandingly and stare at the yellow lenses of his sunglasses.

The young woman who greeted me at the door appears at my side, and her sudden presence would make me flinch if it weren't for feeling like I'm on a David Lynch movie set.

"Follow me, please." The girl leads me off the stage and I follow her, past the rows of women reclining on their velvet chaises.

The farther I walk, the more I transform into an old cartoon character, the one who does something stupid, or trusts too much, and their head morphs into a big candy circle with the word SUCKER, or their ears and nose grow and they turn into a jackass.

I walk through the purple tunnel and see the girl open the door for me. She smiles and nods and I return the gesture, step out onto the sidewalk. As the door shuts with a soft thud behind me, the heavy sensation of being scammed out of four hundred dollars feels like a belly full of cement.

My eyes adjust to the darkened street, but after being in the yellow surroundings, I see a vast purple ocean over everything. I get into the driver's seat of my car and this is when the reality of what I've done hits home. I handed over four hundred dollars to the King of the Pimps in a canary suit, and now I'm supposed to go to some other address—probably some deserted crackhouse— close to midnight, and I have no idea why or for what.

"Goddammit, Mimi." I start my car and grip the steering wheel more tightly than usual. On any other street, I'd drive until I could make right turns, loop around, and go back the way I came. But there's no one driving here. *No one.* I do a three-point turn right in the middle of the street and then hang a left off of Pearl and back onto Main Street.

Four hundred dollars for a scribbled note and a key. Fire sale of the year, Caroline. Good job. Way to keep it together.

I get home, walk inside my house, set my purse and keys down. The sound of my keys hitting the table in the foyer is startlingly loud in the quiet of my house, but I ignore it and head for the kitchen.

I keep a bottle of Smirnoff vodka in my freezer for certain moments, certain *days*, and this is certainly one of them. I withdraw the frosted bottle and grab a glass from a cupboard, pour myself two fingers worth. It's all I allow myself. I used to drink wine, enjoyed it a lot actually, but now I keep alcohol at a distance. It would be too easy to use it to numb the little feelings I have left. Today is a bit of a struggle, but I force myself to put the bottle of vodka back in the freezer.

The icy liquor is a beautiful duality as I swallow. The chilled vodka hits my stomach and I feel the burn flow through me. I don't know what I want for dinner, don't know if I even *want* to eat, and I take my glass with me as I walk into the living room and sit down.

Five visits, fourteen minutes each. You'll know what to do.

"What the hell does that mean?" My whispered question seems loud in the living room.

I glance at Bobo. He's giving me the side-eye.

"We're gonna keep tonight just between you and me, okay? We shall never speak of it again, Bobo."

I take a drink, lean my head back, and close my eyes. My mind drifts to the night I gave the teddy bear to Emma.

⁓⁓⁓

It was bedtime and I had read *The Giving Tree* by Shel Silverstein. Emma's eyelids looked heavy, and I pulled her blankets up over her chest to tuck her in.

"Oh! I forgot your surprise!"

"A surprise?" Emma smiled at me, and I melted inside.

I nodded and went to my bedroom to retrieve the stuffed animal I had hidden. I held it behind my back as I entered Emma's room again and presented it in front of me.

"I got you a bedtime buddy! Gotta think of a good name for him though."

Emma's smile grew wider. She studied his face for a moment and then squeezed him tightly with both arms. "His name is Bobo!"

I leaned closer, touching my nose to Emma's, and whispered through a smile. "That's a good name. I love you so sooooo much."

"I love you too, Mommy." For a moment, the three of us—Me, Bobo, and Emma—are a sandwich as Emma wraps her arms around my neck for a monster hug, squishing the stuffed animal between us. "Thank you. I love him, and Bobo will protect me."

I sat up straight, wondering if there had been any drills at school I didn't know about, something meant to keep kids safe in an emergency, but also puts a new fear into their minds. "Protect you from what, baby?"

"The Birdman."

I ran through my mental inventory and found no reference whatsoever to a Birdman.

"Who's the Birdma—"

"He looks in my window sometimes at night. When Daddy was here, the Birdman used to stay away, but now . . . " Emma's happy expression faded. Her smile wilted and she averts her eyes.

My stomach flipped as I listened to Emma. I turn to look at her bedroom window and see the neighboring house and the night sky.

"Well . . . Bobo is gonna do a great job protecting you, know that?" I put my hands beneath her armpits and gave her a brief tickle, which always makes Emma's face open up with sunshine and laughter. She squealed and I stopped right after, pulled her blankets back into place, and adjusted Bobo so he's in her arms. "Get some sleep, Sunshine, okay?"

She yawns a nod and closes her eyes. I sat there a while longer, watching her face relax. Her tiny Cupid lips parted as she slipped into sleep. I'm raging inside. I want to call her father, scream at him, curse him, make a voodoo doll, and shove pins deep inside the burlap figure until his insides rupture, for leaving and making Emma feel unsafe.

⁓⁓

The sound of a glass thumping against the carpet makes me snap my head up from the couch and I look at my empty hand, chilled but absent of vodka. My head is foggy and I realize I've drifted off for a while. It takes an effort to avoid looking at the photographs of Emma, but I thankfully succeed and check the digital clock on the cable box beside the TV.

11:08 PM

I remind myself that vodka is clear and won't stain the carpet, pick up my fallen glass, and shuffle to the kitchen to set it in the sink. It's not quite the time I usually go to bed, but today has been nothing if not an absolute obliteration of routine. I flick off the light and pause at the threshold between kitchen and living room.

Bobo sits there, his obsidian, glassy eyes staring at me, from the *opposite side* of the couch where I left him.

⌇

I have never been a person inclined to believe in the *woo-woo* ideas of the world. I do not believe in reincarnation or Tarot cards or that if we gather to sit in uncomfortable benches once a week and sing songs with terrible lyrics, we'll all exist beyond death in some fluffy-clouded paradise with our dead loved ones. I have always adhered to worm-dirt theory. We live, we die, we get eaten by worms. There is no beyond *this*.

But I'm in my car, the address from the scrap of paper plugged into my GPS, and a brass key in my pocket. I feel like an idiot, but a bit less of one than I did withdrawing four hundred dollars and driving to a movie theatre in the abandoned section of the city.

I did *not* leave Bobo on that side of the couch. I've gone over and over my actions and I'm certain of it. My thoughts want to make a gigantic leap in certain directions, but I won't allow it. Can't even consider them as possibilities.

Yeah, I'm driving out to the middle of nowhere in the countryside. Part of me is grateful for not having to repeat my earlier drive into the sketchiest parts of the city, but I can't help but wonder what wild goose chase I'm on. The GPS tells me I'll get there at 11:52 PM, but I'm not sure I trust the prediction with the winding rural roads I'm driving on.

I'm a half-mile away and all around me, there isn't a single spark of light in the darkness. I can feel the road slanting downward, leading me into a valley. Even beneath the sleeves of my jacket, the hair on my arms stands up as a chill ripples through me. There's a feeling here as I descend into the thickly wooded area like hungry eyes are watching from a distance, expecting an offering of some kind.

I haven't seen a mailbox or driveway in miles. But I do now.

I bring my car to a stop in the road, letting the glow of my headlights remain on the edge of a gravel path. A thick post with a dented silver mailbox shows the address number. I ease my foot off the brakes and turn into the drive, hearing the rocks crunch beneath the tires. To my left is a farmhouse that didn't fare well with a fire—even in the light of my headlights, I can see the black smoke damage on the faded clapboard, fanning out and widening like massive exclamation marks from the first-floor windows. The upper half of the building is gone, leaving the remains like a tooth rotted off at the gums.

What's left of what used to be a large barn is farther left, and even the thick timber skeleton inside has partially fallen down. In the shine of the car's headlights, it appears like ancient ruins.

To the right of the house sits a squat shack about the length of a trailer, and twice as wide. Above a large plate-glass window is a sign that reads: CHUY'S FIX-IT-UP HUT in thick white paintbrush strokes. Strips of blue tape zigzag over the glass window like a lightning bolt. Weeds surround the building, and by the looks of the wild roses and raspberry bushes along the side of the shop, it's been vacant for quite some time.

I park the car and shut off the engine. When I get outside, I hear chirping crickets and nothing else. There's a faint smell in the direction of the house, ghost whispers of charred wood and pain.

Using the flashlight on my phone, I walk to the front of the building, to the door on the side. I step over a spiky branch of a raspberry bush onto a cement slab and fish the key from my pocket.

It doesn't fit the lock.

"What the actual . . . " I grit my teeth, turn away, and walk along the length of the trailer to the rear. A rain gutter has fallen away from the side, angled down to the very end of the building, and I hop over a patch of mud and stare at the wooden door covered with peeling flakes of white. To the right of it is a small yellow crown on the gray siding, and seeing that symbol here, out in the countryside, makes the hair stand up on my arms.

I try the key on the brass lock. It slides in and I turn the key, listening to a deadbolt slide back. When I open the door, all I see from side to side are tall racks stacked with piles of assorted pieces and parts of appliances. The walls are rough-cut lumber, like the walls of an old farm shed. It smells slightly of turpentine and gas cans, oil and grease.

I shine my light around as I take cautious steps. Shelves of vacuum cleaners and hoses, fans of all sizes, wires dangling from electric motors, washing machines and air conditioners, radios and TV tubes, rabbit ear antennas, columns of VCRs and stereos, and speakers in various states of disrepair.

I make my way through the room to a doorway with long strands of beads hanging from the top of the frame. At one time, the beads must've been shiny metallic purples, greens, and golds, but now they're coated with a dull film of dust and strands of cobweb. I part the beads to walk through, and in stark contrast to the shelves of chaos behind me, I find myself in a small waiting area with a professional-looking shop counter. It's dusty, but bare, save for a short stack of newspapers and a rotary phone on the far end of the counter beside a legal-sized notepad.

Two matching sofas form a capital *L*, with a circular coffee table in front of them. It holds dust-covered magazines—issues of *Hot Rod*, and *Wide World of Wrestling*—and a small TV with a rabbit ear antenna sitting on top, complete with aluminum foil flags at the ends.

There's a plastic toolbox on the floor by the coffee table, with a screwdriver and small hammer beside it. I wonder what the person who left it there was trying to fix.

I check my phone, see it's 11:58, and stand there, adjusting my stance, listening to the grit beneath the soles of my shoes, and the muffled sound of crickets outside.

"I'll know what to do . . . sure. Am I supposed to change careers? Start fixing vacuums and VCRs?" I shine my light on a hanging wall calendar, notice it's from 1986. Cindy Crawford kneels on a beach, grains of perfectly placed sand on her perfect bikinied body.

I sit down on the couch closest to me, watch the dust motes rise, caught in the beam of my flashlight. As much as I feel like novocaine has been injected into my very existence, I suddenly want to cry while I sit here.

It doesn't happen, but I feel like it should.

I'm *angry* at myself, for letting even a small part of me believe, to invest myself into the words of strangers, to let myself be vulnerable to hope. In my mind, I see flash-fire images of Emma, still-frames of so many moments of her life, laughing or doing something cute, and every tenth frame is of her dead body, laying in the weeds.

The tears still won't come. Much like the cactus in my office, they seem to run on a schedule of their own. I let out a heavy exhale, watching the dust swirl and twirl in the air in front of me, and then I stand up, ready to be home in my lonely bed, sobbing in pain or numb to life, ready to pack hope into a small box and toss it aside.

I walk toward the curtain of once-glorious beads and stumble slightly over a broom handle. Gripping the door frame to steady myself, I reach for the beads and stop halfway. Ahead of me in the land of appliance parts, I can see the shadow of the bead curtain against the shelves, but directly in front of me, the shape of my figure is cast on the beads themselves.

Slowly, I turn, and a large eel uncoils inside my stomach, slipping and sliding against my internal organs. The TV emits a harsh glow from its small, static-filled screen, and I watch the image flicker to a black and white waving American flag. The *Star-Spangled Banner* is playing and it sounds both loud and somehow muffled in the room, as if the cheap, moisture-warped wood paneling soaks up the noise.

I'm not a hundred percent certain, but I'm pretty sure that TV stations stopped doing nightly sign-offs a couple decades ago.

I step closer, stand in front of the coffee table, and in the sharp light of the TV, the dust sparkles like microscopic stars. The video of the waving flag is a mismatched loop, and I can see the slight blip when it starts over again.

The national anthem is coming to an end, the long-drawn-out notes, and my mind draws up some memory of me singing it as a kid.

Home . . . of thaaaaaa . . . braaaaaaaaaaaaaave.

The flag flickers. The blizzard of white noise returns. I wonder if that's that . . . if it'll simply pop like a cheap balloon and fade to black.

And I see it—a shift of movement in the TV snow. Behind the static, a silhouette starts to take form, and I stare at it, that slick eel writhing in my guts. The hair on my arms rises on waves of adrenaline. A chill races up my spine and settles in the marrow of my neck bones.

The shape swirls and pools together like quicksilver, and there's no denying it, no possible way I can apply rational thoughts or questions of logic to explain this. It simply is.

"Mommy?"

And right there, in the middle of Chuy's Fix-it-Up Hut, I fall to my knees and sob. The massive walls of a dam have suddenly given way.

***

I'm not sure I can adequately describe the emotion, not sure an actual term for it exists, but I feel it—oh yes, I feel it—through every single fiber of my being. This isn't in my mind, not some cruel construct born of grief and pain meant to soothe the wounds and scars.

That's Emma, my Emma, my Sunshine, on the TV screen in front of me, out in the middle of nowhere, in some abandoned repair shop coated with years of dust and decorated with long-forgotten magazines and calendars of supermodels.

"Su . . . Sunshine?" I feel out of body. My words, the voice, was mine, but not mine.

But her head turns, her ragdoll curls swinging with the motion. Emma's eyes look right at me.

"Mommy? Where are you?" She squeezes her eyes closed, and Emma's cherubic face strains and then crumples like it does when she's on the verge of tears. "It's cold here and I miss you. I miss Bobo . . . "

"Oh Emma . . . oh baby . . . " I crawl over the dirty floor toward the coffee table, let my face bathe in the static glow. "I'm here. I'm here, Sunshine. I miss you so much, baby. *Sooo* so much."

Emma's eyes blink and I see the glistening tears trail down her cheeks, but she looks at me. She sees me, and her mouth shifts into a slight smile.

"Mommy."

"I'm here, baby." I feel my cheeks bathed in tears, boiled hot from months of neglect, but at least I can speak without my voice cracking. "Emma? I see you, can you see me?"

"I see you, Mommy." She nods and her smile grows a little wider. "Where are you?"

"I . . . I'm . . ."

How do I explain this? How the hell do I explain to my dead daughter where I am?

"That doesn't matter, baby. I'm here. I—"

"I'm all alone." Emma turns and looks around. "There's nothing here, Mommy. I don't like—"

"Look at me. Look at Mommy, baby."

She does, her gaze finding me, and I watch as the worry on her face eases a little.

In the back of my mind, I hear a whisper.

Five visits, fourteen minutes a day.

"Baby, listen to Mommy now, okay? I need you to . . . to listen to Mommy like a good girl."

"Okay, Mommy."

"Okay, good. Sunshine . . . what's the . . . what's the last thing you remember?"

No, I have never been religious or superstitious, or a believer in the *woo-woo* . . . but right now, I'm offering a prayer to any god who will listen . . .

Please, please don't let my baby girl's last memory be of how she died . . . of the last moments of her life.

On the TV screen, I can only see her from the waist up, like she's some child star on social media. She looks away from me and tilts her head. Her mouth makes a slight twist, and I recognize her body language immediately—Emma's thinking face.

"I remember kissing you goodbye, and . . . waiting for the school bus, *annnnnd* . . . I looked into my lunch bag to see what you wrote on my note. The Bowen's dog was barking."

"No, no, that's . . . that's good, Sunshine. It's good you remember all that, but do you . . . " I shift, hear the dirt grind on the floor beneath me. "Do you remember anything . . . unusual? You know, anything, um . . . strange?"

"Hmmmmm." Emma rocks back and forth slightly as she thinks. Her eyes are still averted away from me as her mind works, and then her serious expression fades and her face shines like a new lightbulb. "I know, Mommy!"

"What is it, honey? Tell Mommy."

"It was early, before school even, I saw—"

The TV screen snaps and the static changes to a dark black. The only light in the room is the flashlight on my phone.

"No!" I scramble closer, put my hand against the side of the TV. "No, no no, Sunshine!"

The screen fades to a pinpoint of light and I put my face right up close to it, close enough to feel the static tickle my skin. Emma's voice is a whisper so faint it could be a thought.

"Frank. I saw Frank, Momm—"

In the silence, I stay right where I am, keep my hand on the side of the TV until its warmth turns cold again.

———

I didn't set my alarm but it doesn't matter. Even though I'd been awake on the couch until almost three o'clock in the morning, my eyes flick open and I check my phone: 5:17 AM. I realize at some point during the night, I pulled Bobo close to me. His lifeless eyes stare at me and I stare back and then nuzzle my cheek against the side where Emma used to. The fur on this side has been smoothed down, flattened by her love for the stuffed animal, and even though I'm positive it's only in my mind, I think I can smell Emma's scent, faint and distant, like late-blooming wildflowers on an autumn walk.

I lay there, eyes closed, holding Bobo.

Frank. I saw Frank, Momm—

Emma's words in my mind, turning over the names of any neighbors and any kid on the school bus or playground or classroom she's ever mentioned, any teacher or librarian or pet animal she might have seen or known.

But my mind is coming up empty. I lay there on my sofa with Bobo, and keep my eyes closed to the photographs of Emma because I'm not ready to look at them all yet.

The memory of last night threatens to surge up completely and fully, to force me to relive everything second by second, to violently *believe* it all happened and wasn't a dream.

But it doesn't have to, because I already *do* believe.

That was my Emma. My Sunshine.

I listen to the silence of the house, random clicks of settling here and there, the wooden bones expanding and contracting with the temperature. I think of Emma's footsteps upstairs during school mornings, hearing her carefully walk downstairs and show me whatever she had decided to dress in that day.

Last night, Emma was dressed in the same clothes they found her in. It was school picture day and she wore a little white blouse with a black dress over it. It has this tiny turquoise bow on the front. Dainty. Pretty. Emma had me put rag curls in her hair the night before, but she wasn't a little princess, not by a long shot. She could make mud pies with the best of them, capture crickets and grasshoppers, and once, I found out she had kept a toad in a shoebox beneath her bed, giving it water and beetles she picked off the wild fox grape vines behind the house. She took care of that little toad for a full week, and then I made her let it go, back into the wilds of our backyard.

My mind has drifted for a while, and I check my phone for the time, surprised it's almost seven now, and call Scott at the office.

"Good morning, Scott Steele."

"Hey, good morning, Scott. It's Caroline."

I hear the sound of his leather chair creaking as he leans back.

"Hey there. Everything okay?"

"Yeah, oh . . . yeah, it's okay. I think I . . . I'm not going to be in today."

"Sick?"

"No, I just um . . . a little rest and relaxation, I guess."

I hear Scott clear his throat. "Well good. Still gonna need to take a full week though, okay?"

"Oh yeah, of course. I wasn't . . . I'm not trying to wiggle out of it."

"Alright, good. Cindy asked me if you had scheduled it yet. I swear, that woman needs to find a boyfriend, a girlfriend, something with batteries or a hobby."

Internally, I agree with him, but I don't know how to respond, and so I let the silence hang until Scott continues, wishing me a good day off, and hangs up.

The morning light in the living room is dim, and despite knowing what will happen, I open my eyes. Drawn like a moth to a flame, my gaze lands on a photograph of Emma, and as I knew it would, my mind trip-fires into recollecting the circumstance of the picture.

———✳———

A day at the beach in Cape May, New Jersey. I took the picture right after we sat for a while on one of the benches. We were eating boardwalk fries, and then a seagull pooped on my forearm. Emma pointed, her mouth open wide, and then disgust and shock was replaced with giggling. She put a hand over her mouth, trying to stifle her laughter, and then my shock and disgust turned, and I started giggling.

Emma laughed so hard she peed herself, started to get upset until I burst out laughing over the situation. The two of us sat there, bird shit on my arm, and Emma in piss-soaked jeans, laughing our fool heads off until tears streamed down our cheeks.

Our stomachs hurt and heads swam, and we threw away what little fries remained in our cups, used the napkins to wipe the tears off our faces, and the seagull poop from my arm. I tied my hoodie around Emma to hide her wet jeans, and we walked back to the hotel, stopping for intermittent fits of laughter that bubbled up out of nowhere. Hell, I almost peed myself twice on the walk back.

I got her a stuffed seagull before we left Cape May.

Another photo of Emma, dressed up as a cat for Halloween, complete with ears, whiskers, and an eerily lifelike tail. She had a full bucket that night. I remember an old man, unprepared for trick-or-treaters, gave her a Klondike ice cream bar and then turned his porch light off as he shut the door. Despite Emma's protests, I thought an ice cream treat too odd and strange and I stuffed it in a garbage can a few houses down.

Another, Emma in the front yard. Summertime, and I had a sprinkler set up, this little whale that flapped its tail back and forth and spouted water in random directions. In the photo, Emma smiles with clenched teeth as the cold water catches her by surprise. A freeze-frame of her, eyes wide and shining like polished marbles.

We had to rush for some reason. I remember toweling her off in a hurry, and then we ran across the street to . . .

I sit up as my mind tries to dredge something from the muddy depths of memory. My gaze slides from the photograph to the pink box on the bottom shelf of my bookcase. I get up, bring the container back with me and sit it on my coffee table.

Inside, there are stacks of loose photographs. Holidays and school events, three-day weekend trips, or visits to the Touch Museum or the Whitaker Center for Science and the Arts. I pull out a thick stack and flip through them.

I sift through the photos, my mind no longer interested in reliving every memory, focused on finding one specific picture. That day with the lawn sprinkler is bothering me, an itch in an unreachable spot.

Then I see it, see Emma's smiling face, her mouth a smear of color as she holds out a red, white, and blue popsicle toward the camera. I let the other photographs drop into the box.

Behind Emma, in the distance across the street, I stare at the bright blue panel truck with fluffy clouds painted across its surface, stare at the bright, kid-friendly lettering. My hands start to shake, and when I whisper, my voice trembles.

"Frosty Frank's."

⁓⁓⁓

I call the number I found online and a woman answers, her voice aged with years of unfiltered cigarettes. A few politely worded lies in the form of questions, and I got the answer I was looking for.

Hake's Park was a few miles south of me, close to Interstate 83. It was an eight-acre plot of land with a long, curving asphalt path around its edge, and was frequented by runners and walkers at any time of day. Playground equipment draws the kids in like flies. There's an elaborate monkey bars leading to a jungle gym and rope bridges, all of it nestled in a thick wooden frame filled with rubber mulch. The park is taken care of as well if not better than most high-end golf courses.

When I pull into the parking lot, I see a man opening the hatchback of his Subaru and a yellow Labrador jumped out, excitedly wagging its tail. An elderly couple holds hands as they step from the grass onto the asphalt path. It's cute how they're wearing matching jogging suits, and it makes me smile and sad at the same time.

I park my car and turn the ignition to OFF. The clock on my dash reads 11:44 and I let out a slow exhale.

Frank. I saw Frank, Momm—

I hear the music from far away, but I recognize it immediately as the ice cream truck, the same twinkling music box song that makes every child within earshot ask for money.

I watch the painted truck pull into the lot and stop on the right side, away from parked cars. The side door slides open and I watch the man, Frank, step outside, lift up a panel on the truck to form a small portico. He locks it in place with rods and looks around the parking lot.

Adults and children both walk toward the ice cream truck. I pick up the bright yellow MISSING flyer from my passenger seat, fold the paper backwards on all sides until it's cropped down to only the photo of Emma.

The parking lot is crushed stone, and I watch small puffs of dust rise up from the footsteps of the people in front of me. I'm eighth in line, and I listen to people's orders of Drumsticks or Orange Cream Bars, Rocket Pops, and Choco Tacos. More people line up behind me, chatting and murmuring, but they're all white noise. My attention is focused.

I watch Frank move inside the truck, hear him sliding freezer doors open, and I study his movements as he grabs napkins and hands them and the treats in one smooth motion to the customers.

The boy in front of me walks away holding his chocolate chip cookie sandwich, and I step close to the counter, holding out the flyer in my hands so Frank can see.

"Do you recognize this little girl?"

He looks at me, glances down at the photo for less than a second, and then back to my face. "Lady, I sell about four-hundred ice creams a day. Do you have any idea how many kids I see that look just like her?"

"Yes . . . I understand that, but could you—"

"Look, there's a line waiting. Are you gonna buy ice cream, or . . . ?"

I stare into his eyes, lean against the counter. His gaze flits down to the revolver sticking from my purse, and his eyes widen. My voice drops lower, and though I feel my stomach shiver inside, I sound steady as a rock.

"Take another look, a *goooood, lonnnng* look. Do you recognize her?"

Frank is still locked on my eyes and I see the fear there, bright as road flares. He slowly plants the palms of both hands onto the counter, as if to show he's not going to do anything stupid. I wave the flyer slightly, and he stares at it, really takes it in.

I know what he's going to say before he says it. I've been watching his expression, his eyes, the entire time. There's not an ounce of recognition.

"Lady, I'm really sorry for whatever's going on, I truly am, but I really don't think I've ever seen that little girl, okay?"

I unfold the flyer, smooth it out and leave it on his counter. "If you remember anything, there's a number to call."

I glare at him a moment longer, hoping for some poker player tell in his face to indicate he's lying. But there is nothing in his eyes, nothing hiding in the shadows.

"Would you like some oatmeal raisin cookies?"

I do a slow blink at Darren, partially because he seems to have materialized out of thin goddamned air as soon as I pulled into my driveway, but mostly because asking me this question to greet me is . . . odd.

Darren is holding a plastic-wrapped bundle of what appears to be cookies in one hand and a bulging canvas tote bag in the other. It has a silk screened image of a pair of hands, praying, with a large cross behind it.

"I, um . . . " I don't even remember if I like oatmeal raisin cookies. "That's really nice of—"

"You doing okay, Caroline?" Darren's expression is empathetic to the edge of being condescending. On his family-sitcom-dad face, it comes off as insincere, and oddly I feel a white-hot flash of anger course through me and then subside just as quickly.

"I'm okay. I—"

"I know the past few months have been—"

"Cold shit served on a hot plate?"

"Oh, that's . . . " Darren reacts as if I slapped him. No, that's too far. He reacts as if I goosed him or told him something too personal. His shocked face shifts to something else, back to his awkward normality.

"That's one way to . . . " He chuckles nervously. "I know it's been a rough time and I . . . "

Darren averts his eyes to the driveway beneath his brown-loafered feet. "I just . . . I like you, Caroline. I *care* about you. If you ever need, you know, to vent or whatever, I'm . . . I just want you to know I'm here. For you. If you ever want to maybe get a cup of coffee or . . . come over for dinner, or . . . " Darren exhales slowly as if he's unburdened something he's kept inside for a long while.

"Oh. *Ohhhhh*." It hits me. "Oh, Darren, I . . . "

I do *not* have a poker face. I am undecided if that's a blessing or a curse, though at times in my life it's been both. There is zero doubt in my mind Darren reads my expression immediately. A faint blush of pink spreads through his face, and if Darren wasn't . . . Darren, I might find his shy, humble approach flattering, or at the very least, amusing. But I cannot shake the feeling every time we talk, there should be a canned laugh track or the occasional audience-wide *awwwww* in the background.

"Yeah, Darren, I'm . . . I know you're here, *annnnnd* I appreciate it. I do."

I have to get out of here, away from this conversation. I hook a thumb toward my house. "I've got a . . . a thing I have to—"

"Yeah, of course, sure." He shakes his head slightly and holds up the cookies again. "I've got to run anyway. Delivering some things for the baked goods sale at church."

"Of course."

Darren offers the bundle of cookies in my direction once more, and I take them this time.

"Thank you, that's . . . kind of you."

The color on his cheeks deepens. "Very welcome. Anyway, you have a good evening, Caroline. Sorry for . . . sorry."

He mumbles as he quickly walks away toward his car, swinging his tote bag of baked goods like a Pope carrying incense down a church aisle.

I get inside, set my purse down, and stand in the foyer, my back against the front door, and listen to the quiet house. I still expect certain things at times, hearing Emma set her backpack down and turn on the television, the sound of cartoons in the living room.

I expect to hear Emma's laugh or to hear her ask for fruit snacks, or if we can play a game of Go Fish or Candyland. Some mornings, I expect to see her on the sofa, legs tucked up under her t-shirt, sitting there and smiling like some little forest pixie.

At times, it feels like the climb to the top of a rollercoaster, and then the sudden drop right after, the entire sensation in the space of a few heartbeats.

I miss you, Mommy.

I go upstairs to Emma's room, walk inside, and lay down on her bed.

It's a one-room museum of grief in tones of pink and pale yellow. I look at the unicorn poster and the row of small stuffed animals on a wall shelf. From Emma's small white and pink vanity, I see my reflection in the mirror, and I am a giant in her bed. The framed photograph of her on the desk is the last picture ever taken of Emma. I received a packet of them in the mail, three weeks after her body was found, and I can't begin to describe or define what it's like to look at an envelope of school pictures of a dead child, to know you're seeing what she looked like mere hours before she died.

I studied and stared and stared and studied Emma's photo until it was burned into my retinas, until I could close my eyes and still see the lines of her face, her hair, the little bow on her dress.

I turn over on my side, away from the mirror and her photo, and my gaze lands on the wall and a strip of red ribbon tied to a silver bell. I remember the night I tacked the nail into the drywall and hung it for Emma, to protect her from the Birdman.

The bad dreams had gone on for two weeks, waking Emma, crying out for me. I pulled her into bed with me the first week, but her nighttime aerobics kept me awake and I turned into a sleepless zombie during the day.

The Birdman is watching me!

I had taken the bell from a box of Christmas ornaments and tacked it to the wall, told Emma to ring it hard and loud and it would scare away the Birdman. I had absolutely no idea where the source for the bad dreams had come from—no movie or book came to mind, and I racked it up to Emma's imagination. Kids are like that sometimes. I went through a time when I was eight where I was terrified of umbrellas.

I check my phone for the time and see I've got a text message from Alan:

That wasn't fair of you at all, Caroline. I know you're hurting, but I am, too.

I thumb the top of the message screen, navigate to Alan's contact information, and block his number.

I feel so tired right now. Drained.

The box of photographs in the living room used to have pictures with Alan in them. At one point, I sifted them out, panning for Fool's gold, and put them all in a manila envelope with TAX PAPERS scrawled across the front. I sealed it shut and put it in the top of my closet. I suppose I thought even though Alan is an asshole of a man and a terrible father, I kept them in case, at some point, Emma wanted to see them, see something *good* from when she was a baby, see her father smiling and happy.

I guess I can throw them away now.

～

"I'm here, Sunshine."

Emma's gaze focuses, somehow finding me in the glow of the TV screen. Seeing her in black and white is like watching a classic movie. I almost expect her to break out into song.

"Hi, Mommy." Her face breaks into a smile and my heart blooms into confetti.

"*Hiiiii* baby."

"Where did you go, Mommy?"

"I . . . I had to go do some things, but I'm here now." I lean closer to the TV. "Sunshine, did you remember anything else for me? Anything strange?"

"I remember school pictures."

That makes me bite my bottom lip and my throat catches. I nod, take a moment to pull it together. "The pictures are going to look so cute."

That makes her smile wider.

"But do you remember anything else? Closer to . . . um . . . " I catch myself, take a mental step backward and regroup. "Do you remember anything else after that? After getting your pictures taken?"

"I wish Bobo was here. I'm all alone."

My vision is blurred and I blink away tears as I stare at Emma on the TV screen. I swallow hard and clear my throat. "Sunshine, can you do something for me?"

"Yes, Mommy."

"Close your eyes, okay? I want you to close your eyes for me."

Emma hesitates a moment and then shuts her eyes. I see her as I used to see her while she slept, angelic, cherubic, an innocent, beautiful vision of peace. My throat threatens to choke up again, and I press beyond it.

"Good girl, that's my good girl." I scoot closer to the TV so Emma can hear me better. "I want you to think about how Bobo feels when you hug him. His soft, brown fur and how squishy he is."

Her eyes are still closed, but Emma smiles.

"Think of how he smells when you hold him close."

I'm watching the screen, watching Emma, and see a blur in front of her, a smeared vision, and Emma opens her eyes wide and her smile explodes like the sun as she looks down and I watch her draw Bobo up into her arms and squeeze him close.

"Bobooooo!"

This time, my tears build and build and crest the levy of my eyelids. They trickle down my face and hang in hot droplets. I use my forearm to wipe my face and eyes and the TV screen emits a soft, high-pitched pop and whine, and I watch the light fade.

———

It's 3:38 in the morning and I've been awake on the couch in the unlit living room. The real Bobo sits beside me. My phone buzzes and I grab it from the coffee table, check the screen to see a text from UNKNOWN NUMBER:

It might be nothing but talk to Carl Stenson. There are rumors.

I rest my phone on my chest and stare at the ceiling for a long, long while.

———

I've been awake for several hours, and for at least the last half hour I've been staring at the scrap of paper on my coffee table. It has an address written on it, one that took me less than fifteen minutes to find. Carl Stenson.

After some online digging, I found headlines from local news at the top of the search results. Seven months ago, Katie Stenson, daughter of Carl and Jodie, had been playing in the backyard and went missing.

She still hasn't been found.

I wouldn't go so far as to say I know Carl, but we've exchanged smiles and words on many mornings. Even bought him a gift envelope with twenty dollars of scratch off tickets for Christmas last year.

Carl Stenson is the bus driver who took my daughter to school. He looks a bit like Tommy Lee Jones with less wrinkles. Considering he dealt with a busload of elementary school kids every morning and afternoon, I thought him to be one of the calmest, most patient men on the planet. Emma had said he often had the kids singing songs on the bus, and told them a joke in the morning and a riddle in the afternoon.

Apparently, both Carl and Jodie were questioned over Katie's disappearance, but no charges were filed. No evidence of any kind to indicate their involvement. The case was still open, but Katie's disappearance seemed to be racked up to human trafficking.

According to the public record, they filed for divorce two months ago. A week ago, a notice of home foreclosure was posted in the newspaper.

Like I said, I've never been one to believe in the *woo-woo*. I've also never been prone to snippets of fortune cookie advice, but from my life experience, I do believe in one old adage . . . where there's smoke, there's fire.

Carl's house is in a cul-de-sac, two houses from the end. Nice enough neighborhood, but I can tell it's older, designed by the generation of architects who were big fans of *The Brady Bunch*. Tidy lawns and landscaping right up to the sidewalks.

Then, there's *his* house.

It's some kind of step-child of modern Tudor, with wide wooden beams angled and prominent to show the structure of the home, but with tan vinyl siding filling in the spaces. I'm not even sure there's a name for this kind of architectural style because I am damned sure it didn't catch on.

Even from where I park my car, I can see the grass is too high, past my ankles. There's a sheet of paper, taped top and bottom, to the front door, and even I know nothing good is delivered like that. The paint is peeling around the window and door frames, and the corner of the garage looks mossy as if it's starting to rot.

I take a deep breath and walk to the front door, read the FORECLOSURE NOTICE headline on the taped paper. I push the doorbell button, and when I don't hear any ringing inside, I open the glass door and give the main door several hard raps.

There is no yapping of a dog, nor heavy footsteps heading in my direction.

I ease the glass door shut, and walk around the side of the house, toward the rear. The grass swishes against my jeans, making me feel itchy, but I keep going until I reach the corner of the house. There's a cement deck surrounding an in-ground pool that has seen better days. It's filled with pond-brown water and a skim of leaves float on the surface.

Someone issues a harsh, clipped laugh and I flinch toward the source—a man sitting in a lounge chair near a sliding glass door to the house.

I cautiously move closer so I can see the front of him. He stares forward, not even glancing in my direction when I'm plainly in his line of sight. I walk onto the cement pool deck and stop in front of Carl Stenson.

He holds a coffee mug in his right hand, and I notice a fifth of Old Grand-Dad whiskey nestled in his crotch. Carl wears gray sweatpants and a pale blue robe with a stained t-shirt beneath. I turn behind me and see a playset in the backyard. That is what Carl is staring at.

He takes a sip from his mug, and I watch the way he sharply sucks his teeth and flicks his tongue out over his lips after he swallows.

"Carl, my—"

"Fuck you want? Money?" Carl's gaze still hasn't landed on me, but he chuckles and takes another drink of whiskey. "Get in line."

"Not exactly, no. You used to be the bus driver for my daughter."

Carl shifts his focus toward me, and I can see how bloodshot his eyes are—thin lacy lines of red over a yellowed background. "So fuckin' what?"

His words are aggressive, but his tone is not. His voice sounds distant, weakened or diluted somehow, farther away than it should.

"Emma Jacobsen."

Carl stares at me quietly. I watch his chest rise and fall as he breathes slowly, but heavily.

"Emma." He nods. "Girl 'at went miss—" He takes a drink from his mug. "Yeah, I remember her."

Something about his words, no, his tone of voice, makes me bristle. My arms had been crossed, and I realize I'm now gripping the handle of the revolver.

"Yeah . . . I was her bus driver." Carl lifts his mug, pauses and looks inside, and then pours from the uncapped bottle of Old Grand-Dad. He returns the bottle between his legs and takes a drink from his mug.

"I'm . . . I read about your daughter, and I'm sorry for your loss."

Carl erupts into not laughter, but an absolute cackle. He leans over, his laughter evolving into a hacking cough, and he almost drops the whiskey to the cement, does a frantic grab only *real* alcoholics are known for and saves the bottle.

His cough subsides and he shakes his head as if to banish the sensation, and then he straightens up again, red-faced and glassy-eyed. "My loss."

Carl coughs again twice and then taps his chest with a closed fist. "That's rich. My loss."

"My daughter Emma went missing, too. But they . . . they found her later, dead."

And now I talk to her on a fifty-year-old black and white television set. Act now, Carl, and for only $19.99 plus shipping and handling, YOU CAN TALK TO YOUR DEAD DAUGHTER, TOO!

Carl pauses midway during the action of lifting his mug to drink. He's staring at the playset in the backyard, again. "I heard. Your daughter, Emma . . . she was on my bus. Beautiful."

I feel my nostrils flare at his tone of voice. It's not sleazy, but there's desire there. A want of some kind I don't understand, and it makes me queasy. It also makes me adjust the revolver in my grip.

Carl leans his head to the left and then to the right, and I hear a popping sound from his neck. He clears his throat. "She was a great student, you know that? She was. Teachers . . . teachers loved her, they really did. Cute little thing, she was."

My stomach flips and I take a step closer, close enough I can smell the tinge of oak-barrel aged alcohol in the air.

"I remember the little dresses she used to wear, how pretty she was. Her laugh, her laugh was like little silver bells ringing. And her face . . . oh her face, so soft."

I pull the pistol from my purse without thinking about it, and my hand is down at my side. "Carl . . . " Even on a one syllable word, my voice trembles. I take a deep breath and exhale slowly before I begin again. "Carl, what did you do?"

His eyes, already glassy, boil over, and I watch tears run down the cheeks of his face, racing until they reach his gray stubble. His Tommy Lee Jones face tightens, and I can't help but think that now he looks worn and weathered and carries more wrinkles than his look-a-like.

"I'm so tired of questions." His lower lip puckers out, childlike, and he nods, agreeing with his own statement. "Questions from Jodie, from the lawyers . . . from the police. Just over and over and . . . "

Carl coughs loudly, clears his throat, turns his head, and then spits a wad of yellow phlegm to the pavement. "Jodie, over and over . . . questions and . . . always with the fuckin' questions."

I'm breathing heavily, but I don't feel adrenaline pumping through my veins.

"The cops, they say they don't know . . . " Carl lifts the bottle of whiskey and sets it down beside him. He stands up and stuffs his free hand into the pocket of his robe.

His voice lowers to a whisper, speaking to himself. "She was beautiful . . . so, so beautiful." More tears spill down over Carl's cheeks, hanging like dewdrops from his chin.

I slide my finger into the trigger guard of the revolver.

"The cops, they say they don't know who took her, but I do." Carl nods, his lower lip still puckered out. "Oh, I know."

I shift my arms, cross them in front of me at my waist. "Carl?"

"The Birdman. Just picked her up one day and flew away with her."

My stomach flips. "What does that . . . who's the Birdman, Carl?"

His face crumples into an agonized smile. His eyebrows knit and his expression is a surrealist portrait of grief. He swallows hard and then withdraws his hand from the pocket of his robe, a steak knife in his grip.

"Carl?"

Carl opens his mouth and then closes it again. He takes a drink from his mug, pauses, and then takes another swallow. His voice drops to a whisper. "So many questions, just . . . over and over. I'm . . . I'm tired of them. I'm tired."

He drops his mug and I see it fall in slow motion, watch the remaining liquid rise from the container on its descent. The bottom edge of the mug hits first, and I watch it shatter into fragments. The droplets of whiskey follow, painting a rainstorm on the cement.

I raise my gaze to Carl's face and motion returns to real-time.

He raises the blade and draws it quickly across his throat with intent, and I can actually *hear* the Morse Code chatter as the serrated edge bites into the cartilage of his Adam's apple, but then it slices through and is replaced by wet sounds. Deep red cascades down his neck, and I watch the blood spurt free, in sync with his pulse, soaking the neckline of his robe.

Carl lets the blade fall from his hand, and then he drops to his knees. His gaze remains on me for a moment, and then turns to the playset again. Blood rushes from the aggressive slash around his neck, wetting his t-shirt, and Carl lets both arms go slack at his sides. He tries to swallow, unsuccessfully, and blood sputters from his mouth. Carl wobbles slightly, and I think he's going to fall forward, face first onto the cement, but instead, he falls backward. He sprawls onto the cement, his legs bent at an odd, awful angle.

The sky is the palest shade of blue as I walk back to my car.

My eyes are drawn to the Notice of Foreclosure on the front door, and even though I know I should be gone already, should be driving like a bat out of hell to get away from this scene, I'm sitting in the silence of my car.

I pull out my phone and go through my contacts, hit the call button for Liz Brewster, and put it to my ear, listen to the ring, and wonder if there'll be an answer today. I almost end the call on the fourth ring.

"Detective Brewster."

Hearing her voice is like pouring salt on a fresh wound. The police weren't incompetent when Emma went missing. They weren't inept when her body was found. They were just . . . unproductive.

"This is Caroline Jacobsen."

I hear the sound of papers shuffled, and the heavy exhale on the other end.

"Hello, Miss Jacobsen."

I close my eyes and lean my head back against the seat rest. I already know how this conversation is going to go. "I was checking in to—"

"I'm sorry, Miss Jacobsen, there haven't been any updates, but I assure you, if there is anything new, I'll—"

"When."

"Sorry?"

"Not if, Detective. When there's something new." I open my eyes and stare at the sheet of paper taped to Carl's front door. "I mean, people are actually still working on the case, aren't they? Or am I wrong about that?"

I hear another heavy exhale, and the creak of an office chair. "Yes, of course. But, I don't need to explain, after this long, that it's a challenge, but when we find something new, I'll let—"

"I never asked, but do you have kids, Detective?"

There's a hesitancy on her part, and though I might be wrong, I have it in my mind that most cops are private, revealing only what people *need* to know and not much else. "A son, ten."

I nod at her answer. "Kiss him goodnight tonight. Hug him close for longer than you usually do."

The revolver rests in my lap, and I pick it up, turn it one way and then the other to watch the light play along its surface. "I want you to think about how it would feel to never be able to do that again."

I end the call, not bothering to wait for a reply, and stuff the gun back in my purse.

——— ❧ ———

I'm standing over my kitchen sink, eating an oatmeal raisin cookie and drinking a cup of day old, microwaved coffee. I feel lost and uncertain of where to go or what to do next.

Darren has planted flowers along the side of his house, complete with a decorative wire fence to close them in. Stuck into the ground, between two plants, is a small flag with a cross and a bright, shining sun behind it. *He has risen* is printed in block lettering across the top, and I wonder how Darren would react if I asked him if that technically makes Jesus the first zombie.

The sky has darkened from cyan to a muddled gray, and it's dreary. I swallow the last of the cookie and look into the living room. I suddenly cannot be here. The house is quiet except for the wind outside, starting to pick up like a storm is coming. It sounds like the fake whistling wind sound in old black and white movies.

I put my coffee cup on the counter, walk to the hall closet and grab a jacket, and then take my purse as I leave. I'm not even sure where I'm going, but there's a lot of time before I make the drive out to Chuy's later.

Only parents understand the impact having a child has on their lives. Parents are responsible for their child's wellbeing, and that not only pertains to the basics—the whole food, water, shelter stuff—but their actual life. I was with Emma every single day for eight years, six months, two weeks, and three days.

There is literally nothing I can do that doesn't somehow remind me of her. I stop at a gas station and think about how I would sometimes get her a little treat—a ring-pop or sour candy, or once in a while, a candy necklace and bracelet.

I'm driving on a winding back road, passing farmland on both sides. I keep wondering when Emma's going to yell 'Mooooo' or 'Horsie!' from the back seat. I can't stop myself from glancing in my mirror every so often, thinking I'll see her there, but I only find the top of an empty booster seat.

Sometimes we'd sing on drives. "Wheels on the Bus", or "Rudolph the Red Nosed Reindeer" , even if it was the middle of summer. Emma didn't care; she just liked the song. She would giggle each and every time I sang "like a light bulb" after "had a very shiny nose" and it made me laugh along with her. But her favorite, the most sung song by Emma and I, was "You Are My Sunshine". She knew the words by heart, had sung them so many times she knew just where to pause and when to belt it out loud and proud.

My Sunshine.

Somehow, I've arrived here, and I'm not sure how. I slow to a stop at the red light and stare straight ahead at the stretch of asphalt. My gut twists, and I almost roll the window down, afraid I'm going to taste Darren's oatmeal raisin cookie a second time.

The feeling passes and the light turns green. I drive through the light, straight ahead, and I pull off onto the shoulder of the road. I put the car in park, and turn off the ignition.

This is it. This is where they found my Sunshine. This isn't the first time I've been here. I came out once before, about a month after it happened, sat here in my car and bawled until I had to open the door and throw up on the roadside.

I leave my purse in the car and get out. It's the edge of Autumn, and the weeds along the down-sloping bank are starting to lose their bright green and wither to tan. The gravel crunches as I walk closer to the bank.

Right here is where they found her, completely by accident. A young couple got a flat tire and pulled over onto the shoulder, saw her down in the weeds.

I step over the guardrail, onto the grass and then I turn sideways and make my way down the hill, careful not to lose my balance, and reach the bottom. From down here, I can't even see the road. Even if I screamed my loudest, I don't think anyone would hear me.

Trash has either blown down or been tossed into the ravine. Soda cans and beer bottles, and bits of paper and cardboard. A rusted-out barbecue grill lay on its side. There are several bundles of dried flowers, still in cellophane, and I wonder who put them here.

I sit down in the weeds and put my hands into my jacket pockets. My right hand draws out two familiar shapes, and I look at the pack of Marlboro Lights and a small green lighter.

I was going to quit as a promise to Emma, and I guess I kept it, at least after she died.

I know what's inside the box . . . a single stale cigarette. I flip the lid back with my thumb, an action I've done countless times, and shake the Marlboro loose, raise it, and pinch it between my lips. After stuffing the empty box back in my jacket pocket, I cup the lighter in both hands, light the cigarette, and take a long draw. That light-headed nicotine rush hits me, and I can't help but smile a little and nod at the feeling.

The cops didn't tell me when they found her here. I wasn't even called until they had gone through the crime scene and had transported her to the morgue. That was surreal. Being asked to identify your child's dead body on a metal table, that's . . . that's something on TV, something you watch in a movie.

Until it isn't.

When they drew the sheet back from her face, I wanted to rip it out of their hands and pull it back. I wanted to see what had happened to my Emma, what some sick son of a bitch had done to her, how he'd hurt her, what he had . . .

But I didn't. I wanted to, but I didn't. I stared at my Sunshine's face, ran my hand over her head and hair one last time, and nodded that it was her.

I started building the stone tower right afterward. Rock by rock, I made a high stone tower inside me, fairytale straight and tall, so tall its peak sat in clouds.

The thing with walls though, they protect as well as imprison.

I flick ashes with my thumb automatically—little gray flecks catch on an air current and I watch them float and then rush away from me in the wind. To my left, almost hidden behind a reach of weeds, I see the upper edge of a culvert pipe. I stand up and walk closer, see the pipe is almost as tall as I am. It runs beneath the road and I see tan grass in the circular frame on the other side. I hear a faint whistling, and I step directly in front of the pipe, feeling the air tunnel rush over me.

It dies down, and then a blast of wind comes out. I step to the side, out of its direct path, and take another drag off my cigarette. I exhale and watch the smoke curl and twist like ghosts dancing in the wind, away from the bank and pipe and toward a line of tall holly trees.

The cigarette tastes like shit, but I take one last drag anyway, and then I see it, a soft flutter of motion toward the top of the holly tree closest to me. I walk closer and strain my eyes to focus on the darkness behind the tightly knit branches. There's movement there, but I can't tell what it is.

I stub out the Marlboro beneath my shoe, grinding it into the dirt, and then I look around the base of the trees, focusing on a broken branch around eight feet long. I go after it, pick it up, and then, standing as close as I can to the holly tree, I swing that branch, for all it's worth, toward the top of that tree.

And it begins to snow.

⚬⚬⚬

Detective Brewster looks tired. She looks worn and frustrated that I'm here, standing in front of her desk. But I don't give a damn.

"Miss Jacobsen?"

"Katie Stenson."

She clears her throat and holds her hand out, motions for me to sit down. I hesitate, and when she speaks, it's in that *placating a child* tone that I absolutely loathe.

"Miss Jacobsen, please sit down."

I feel hot inside, and I want another cigarette, a fresh one, but I grit my teeth and sit.

Detective Brewster leans on her desk, speaks in a low voice, I'm guessing in an effort to get me to lower mine. "What about Katie Stenson? I know the case, but I didn't work it."

"Are there any similarities between Katie and Emma?"

"You read about her in the news?"

"I did."

She stares at me a moment and then straightens away from her desk. "Then you know everything the public knows."

"And the Birdman? Has anyone asked Carl Stenson about . . . "

My chest seizes right then and there, and through my rage, I realize I need to shut the fuck up. I have not thought this through. What was I going to say? That Carl Stenson says the Birdman took his little girl? That Emma had mentioned the Birdman to me and I just fucking ignored it as her imagination?

Whose girl, Detective?

Oh, the one I talked to earlier, who cut his own throat right in front of me. Oh, right, right! Forgot to call you guys about that. Ooopsie!

"I'm sorry, Birdman? Miss Jacobsen?"

I'm trembling. I close my mouth and look down at my hands in my lap. I shake my head softly, and the anger in me drifts away like stale cigarette smoke on a solid breeze. "Nothing. I'm . . . I'm sorry I bothered you."

I stand up and walk away before I can see the expression I know is on her face. That sympathetic, *she's lost her mind* expression.

⌘

It's a little early, but I'm at Chuy's Fix-It-Up shop. I'm leaning against my car, listening to the quiet out here. In the distance, I hear a cow bellow every so often. The ever-present crickets sing in the darkness.

I am unsure what to ask Emma tonight. I don't know where to go from here, and I can't help but wonder if I don't find answers, does that mean Emma will be stuck forever in whatever place she's in, like some kind of purgatory?

I think of the holly trees, the upper section, so densely packed. In my mind, I can see the dove feathers erupt when I hit it with the branch. I watch them rain down, get caught in the air current from the culvert pipe, and most of them, like barn swallows returning to the nest, float and swirl and return right back into the waiting arms of the holly tree.

My phone buzzes and I check the screen: Liz Brewster.

My heart used to skip when I saw the detective's name on my phone. I always hoped it would be *the* call, the one that would tell me they found who did it. After a while, that false hope heartbeat stopped. My stone tower prevented it from happening.

It's late for a detective to be calling, but I'm early tonight, so I answer.

"Hello, Detective."

"I'm sorry for calling so late."

"It's okay, I'm awake. What's up?"

"Since you came to see me earlier, it's been on my mind. Is there something else, Caroline?"

I consider her words, think about the domino effect of what could happen if I tell her everything. "Nothing else. I was . . . I was confused is all. I haven't been sleeping very well."

"Mmmmhmm. Well, it feels like you're hiding something, and that bothers me, but what bothers me even more is something I can't put my finger on, like something I can't remember just yet."

I let her fishing bait move right past me, and don't reply.

"You referred to him as Carl. You know him?"

"He . . . yeah, he was Emma's bus driver."

I listened to her slow, easy breathing on the other end of the call.

"You have a good night, Miss Jacobsen."

I check my screen to make sure the call has ended, and then put the phone in my pocket.

Inside, I make my way through the building and into the front of the shop. I give a nod to Cindy Crawford, but she ignores me. I turn off my flashlight and wait in the darkness. There's a faint sound of scratching somewhere, mice fluffing a nest, maybe.

I hear a high-pitched whine as the TV screen comes on, and I watch the flickering video loop of the waving flag. Tears come to my eyes as it nears the end, and I get a rushing wave of that lost feeling again. I shake my head and wipe my eyes as I see Emma come into view. She holds Bobo down at her side and smiles at me.

"Hi, Mommy!"

"Hi, baby. I . . . " Her face is so bright and happy, I don't want to continue, but I know tomorrow is our last visit together and time is of the essence. That reality makes me want to break in half, shatter to small grains of dust and join the rest on the gritty floor beneath my feet.

"Sunshine, I have to ask you something very important."

"More important than brushing my teeth?"

She grins as she asks the question, and I cannot help but smile back at her.

"More important than brushing your teeth."

"Mmmmm . . . more important than the Easter Bunny and Santa Claus?"

"More important than them, too."

Emma squeezes the Teddy bear and then nods at me. "Okay, Mommy."

I swallow the lump trying to close off my throat. "Emma, do you . . . do you know what happened to you?"

"I died."

My eyes lock open, staring at her, and I'm afraid to blink. I cannot blink because tears will never stop running down my face. "Do you . . . " I shift in place on the couch, lean closer to the TV. "Sunshine, do you remember how?"

"I don't know. I went to school and . . . when I woke up, I was here."

"Do you remember when you were scared of the Birdman, baby?"

Emma looks away from me and then shakes her head softly. Her eyes look glassy, upset because she can't answer me.

"It's . . . honey, it's really important. It's . . . " I exhale slowly as I sink back against the dusty sofa. I am depleted. I can't do this. I won't be able to get the answers I need. "I'm not mad at you, Sunshine. It's okay. We can talk about something else."

"Umm . . . if you could be any animal, what would it be?"

Despite how I feel, I smile at Emma's game. It's one we played often. "You first, Sunshine."

"Guess!" She says the word excitedly, with a happy little hop.

"A camel?"

"No!" Emma smiles wide.

"You sure? You could carry around all that water in a big hump on your back, and—"

"Nope! Not a camel!"

I tilt my head, pretending as if I'm thinking very hard. "I think maybe . . . a hippopotamus."

"*Noooooo, Mommy!*" This time, there's a giggle with her smile.

"Not a hippo? You could waddle around with big puffy cheeks and a silly smile."

"*Noooo* hippos!"

She's smiling, hands on her hips, with Bobo beneath one arm.

"I give up . . . what animal would you be?"

"An octopus." Her voice lowers, almost shy in her delivery.

"A squishy little octopus? *Ewwwww, whyyyyyy?*"

"So I could have more arms to hug you with!" Emma does that happy little jump again, and I want to scoop her up like I did when she was alive. Lean down and nuzzle against her neck and feel her arms around me and pick her up and hug her tight.

But I can't. And so, I close my eyes, build little dams against tears building up again.

"Do me a favor, Mommy."

"Anything, Sunshine."

"Think of how it feels when I hug you."

"I am, baby. I am."

And I feel cool, smooth arms reach around my neck and squeeze. I stay like that for a moment, reveling in the sensation, and then it abruptly pulls away from me.

Emma has her thinking face on, and I can tell something's troubling her.

I sit up straight and lean down so the glow of the screen is on my face. "Yes, baby? What is it?"

She's not looking at me as I watch her eyes turn glassy, her lower lip pucker out slightly. Emma's trying to be brave, trying to not get upset. She hugs Bobo tighter and then looks at me.

"I told you he was real."

I hear the pop and crackle of the TV screen as it begins to fade to black. "No!" I slap the side of the plastic and then jerk back away from it all. The flashlight of my phone shines straight up, as I've set it on the small table the television is on.

"Who's real?" I stand up and I'm not tired anymore as anger rolls through me like thunderclouds. "The Birdman?"

I grab the cushions from the couches and throw them against the wall. I lunge toward the dusty glass counter and sweep everything off, hearing it crash to the floor among the other debris. I charge through the beaded curtain and try to knock over the shelf to my left, but it doesn't budge. I may as well be pushing a brick wall. I spin to my right, shove the rack of spare parts, and it rocks slightly. I rear back and put all my strength into it, and the shelf teeters at its balance point a moment, and then falls backward with a crack of plastic and metal against the floor.

"The Birdman isn't fucking real!" I scream into the confined space, and the walls, the ancient dust-caked items, group together to eat the noise. This makes me angrier because I want to rage into the world. I want to unleash wrath on whoever did this to my Emma, on myself for having a fling and being a young, dumb woman. On Alan for leaving, for unplugging as a man, as a father.

I want to deliver vengeance.

Tears of anger flow down my face as I kick and scuff at things on the floor, even though I can only make out blurry gray shapes in the dim light. I move to the next shelf and grip the vertical metal supports, hold onto them and force myself to breathe more slowly.

Tomorrow will be the last visit for Emma and me.

No. That's not enough time. That can't be the last time.

I stopped at an ATM and withdrew four hundred dollars, and when I park my car outside the abandoned theatre, I glare at the yellow crown as I walk to the front door and rap my knuckles against it.

It's a little after one in the morning. I know it's late, but I don't care. I'll knock until someone answers. I'll break the goddamn door down if I have to.

But I hear locks being turned from the other side, and the same girl as last time opens the door a crack, and then waves me inside with a smile, almost as if she was expecting me.

When I enter the theater itself, I see all of the chaise lounges are gone, but the women are still there. All of them are dressed in different styles of crimson ball gowns long enough to reach the floor. All have their hair done up and wear a simple pendant hanging from their slender necks.

Each of them is frozen in different postures. Their unblinking eyes stare ahead at nothing.

I'm led through the maze of living mannequins and the feeling is otherworldly, like walking through Hades. Once again, I step onto the stage, to the man sitting on his throne, as fresh and awake as if this was the middle of the day.

He shifts in the chair, turns his head toward me. "Returning the key before your time is up? That's a surprising—"

"No, I'm not returning the key. I . . . I have one visit left."

He tilts his head down, and the fedora hat shadows his face. "Mmmm. I see."

"I don't think you do. You . . . once more isn't enough. It's . . . there's not enough time for me to—"

His outburst of laughter cuts my sentence short, and he lifts his head as if he's speaking to the unmoving crowd of women in front of him. "Not enough time. There's *never* enough time."

"Please listen, I . . . " I pull out the wad of twenty-dollar bills from my pocket, offer it over to him. "I'll pay again if you'll just—"

He snickers, but it's without humor and shakes his head. "You bring me a suitcase o' money, still can't change the way t'ings are."

He stands up from the chair, and I notice he holds a waist-high cane, a twisted length of yellow swirls. On a table to his right, the man picks up a simple goblet and takes a drink of its contents.

His casual response makes my entire body tense and tighten and flood with fresh anger.

"I told you, it's always the same . . . " He tilts his head back, sniffing the air like a hound, and whispers. "Can smell the grief on you like French perfume. Comin' off you in waves."

"I need to know who—"

"You need to accept that sometimes we don't get the answers we seek, no matter how much we want them. Death and sorrow have been lovers a long, long time. Their embrace is eternal, and they keep their secrets close to their heart."

"Stop. Just stop it with your . . . " I feel the revolver in my hand and see myself point it at him before I know what I've done. "Once more . . . isn't . . . enough."

I use my thumb to pull back the hammer of the revolver, and the heavy clicking noise is the only sound in this enormous room.

He smiles at me, takes a drink from his goblet, and returns it to the table.

"Strange is the night where black stars rise." Slowly, he removes his hat and puts it on the chair. "And strange moons circle through the skies."

Looking in my direction, he lifts his hands and removes his yellow sunglasses. "But stranger still, is Lost Carcosa."

His smile widens to a grin. His eyes are absent, replaced by craters of scarred flesh. A ragged horizontal line crosses his face from temple to temple, a wake of destruction. He tilts his head at me like a curious dog.

"You wanna pull the trigger, go on then. Get it over with." He takes a step toward me, leaning down so his face is in line with the barrel of my revolver. "Can't give you what I can't give. You ain't been cheated, got just what I said you was gonna get."

"I'll do it." My hand shakes, and I grit my teeth.

He smiles, showing wide, yellowed teeth. "Whatchoo gonna do wid a handful o' snakes?"

The revolver collapses in my hand, rubber grip and steel trigger changing to a writhing ball of silk rope, and I see the knot of arrow-shaped heads and flicking tongues. I sling it to the stage and watch the snakes crawl over one another, and the man bellows laughter loud enough to echo from the forty-foot high ceiling.

He leans down and I watch a group of heads raise in unison, taste his fingertips with forked tongues, and then he clutches the bundle in his hand. The scaled black skin and pale bellies merge as he straightens up again, and I see he's pointing the gun at me.

"Gimme your fuckin' purse, bitch." He laughs, deep from in his chest, and shakes his head. Taking a step forward, he lets the gun spin downward on his index finger, offering the weapon to me.

I hesitate, waiting for it to change into a group of scorpions or a cluster of spiders.

"Go on."

He nods, his sightless eye sockets aimed in my direction, and I cautiously take the pistol from his hand, stare at the revolver as if it'll betray me, and then stuff it in my purse. Clearly, it's of no use to me.

"My eyes were taken from me when I was young, long before I could see the world as a man, and enjoy the many, many pleasures it offers to be seen." He tucks his sunglasses into an inner pocket of his suit, leaving me no choice but to look at his scarred face.

"But when one sense is taken away, the others rise up to fill the void. I see t'ings, many t'ings, others do not." He points at me, smiles with amusement, and shakes his hand. "But you, with all your senses, can't hear me. I don't make the rules . . . not on this. E'ryone gets what they get, and ain't nothin' I can do 'bout it."

"But she . . . she can't tell me who—"

"You still not listenin' to what I say. We get . . . what we get . . . and that is all." He walks to his throne and sits down, retrieves his hat, and rests it back on his head. "Go on wit' you now. Go finish what business you have and be done wit' it best you can."

As numb as I was when they found Emma's dead body, I am more so as I walk out of the theater. I am absent and void. I am a vacuum, a big empty, without even the weight of my stone tower to hold me in place.

I'm home now, parked in my driveway.

I have absolutely no recollection of getting here.

<hr>

My vibrating phone wakes me from a deep sleep, and I frantically grab it off the coffee table to answer it.

"Good morning, Miss Jacobsen."

The detective's voice jolts me awake and I sit up. "Yes?"

I slip into feeling hope all over again, waiting to hear her tell me they got the person who took Emma, found them and have them locked up.

"That thing that was bothering me yesterday? I remembered."

I say nothing. I notice my purse is on the coffee table and the revolver is lying beside it, though I have no memory at all of taking it out.

"Oh."

The detective was silent on the other end of the call, letting the quiet spool out, waiting for me to fill it. I didn't.

"Never did find Katie Stenson, dead or alive."

"That's awful."

"It is. Like I told you, I didn't work the case, but I hear it's been pretty rough on the parents."

"Yeah, I bet it has."

I hear what sounds like the detective taking a drink of something, and I stand and walk toward the kitchen, heading for the coffee pot.

"Thing is, I talked to the detective who did work the case, who's still working it, and he told me something very interesting, something odd, but not of any real consequence."

"Yeah?" It's coming, I know it is.

"When the Katie Stenson case was being investigated, the detective found drawings in her room. Simple crayon drawings, rainbows and unicorns, and things, but also of a monster with birds flying all around him." She clears her throat and lets out a slow breath.

"That detail wasn't released to the news media. Anything you want to tell me, Miss Jacobsen?"

"Not really, no. I just . . . like I told you, I haven't been sleeping well lately."

"An odd coincidence then, you mentioning a . . . *Birdman?*" Detective Brewster lets her question hang in the air. "A detective is going to check in with Mr. Stenson, go over a few details again, see if anything else has come back to him."

I pull the coffee pot, move toward the sink, and pause, speaking with an edge to my voice. "I know I only asked you yesterday, Detective, but anything new on who killed my daughter? Breaking down any doors? Closing in on any hot new leads?"

I hear another heavy exhale and the call ends.

As I fill the pot with water and scoop coffee into a fresh filter, I process the call. It takes about half a minute before I realize I have to get out of the house. When Carl Stenson's body is found, I have zero doubts I'll get a visit next.

Dumb. That was dumb going to the station.

I leave the unbrewed coffee and I'm out the door less than a minute later.

⌘

It took me a bit of digging, but I found Jodie Stenson's phone number, listed on a job networking site. I called and listened to a recorded message telling me the number dialed was no longer in service.

I drive to the mid-day hangout of Frosty Frank's. I know I'm acting desperate, grasping at straws, but I *am* desperate—I don't know what else to do and I can't sit still and do nothing at all. I pull into the gravel lot and park my car.

There isn't a line at the ice cream truck. It's almost one o'clock and I'm guessing most of the lunch crowd has shuffled back across the street to the office park, returning to work.

I step up to the window, and Frank is crouched down below the counter, messing with something. When he stands up and looks at me, there's a frozen moment and I see his eyes widen with recognition. He reaches to his right and I see he's picked up a phone and is maneuvering his thumb on the screen, his eyes flicking back and forth from me to the phone.

I put out both hands in an *I come in peace* gesture.

"I apologize for scaring you, but that's not going to happen today."

He pauses, studies me, and then turns his phone around for me to see the numbers 911 at the top of the screen.

"You pull any shit like that again, and I'm calling the cops. I've got my thumb on the call button, yeah?"

"Yeah." I put both of my hands on the counter and speak in a calm voice. "This is going to be an odd question, but do you know anything about . . . a Birdman?"

"What?"

I know how it sounds. It makes me appear insane, asking a stranger this question. But I don't have a choice.

"A Birdman. You ever hear any of the kids talk about—"

"Look lady, I don't know what in the actual fu—"

"Never mind. Thank you."

I turn away from him, stuff my hands in my jacket pockets, and walk back to my car. I slide into the driver's seat and close my door and grip my steering wheel until my knuckles turn white. And then I scream and scream and scream.

⌘

A few years ago, Emma and I used to go to a park on Saturday afternoons. It cost a dollar to buy some food from the vending machines, and feeding the ducks was a cheap way to have fun. The two of us would sit on a bench close to the pond, and as soon as Emma would put the money in the machine and the brown kibble would rattle down into the slot, there would be a gaggle of ducks waddling onto the bank and headed toward us.

I showed her how to put a single piece of food in her flattened palm, tuck her thumb in and let a duck snack from it. She would giggle every time she felt a duck's bill snatch it from her hand.

I'm here at the park today, but the machine for duck food is empty. It's all right though, I don't much feel like feeding them alone.

One last visit with Emma. Fourteen minutes.

And then what?

I stare out over the calm water, its surface smooth as glass. For some reason, it makes me think of late nights with Emma when she was a baby. Middle of the night feedings, I'd wake up, shuffle to her crib and hold her against my shoulder while I mixed up formula and threw a bottle in the warmer. It wasn't expensive, and though it somehow seemed extravagant when I bought it, the appliance that eventually came to be known as The Sizzler, was one of the best things I ever got.

Emma would curl against my shoulder as I rocked back and forth and sang any songs I could remember, and after a minute or two, the bottle would be warmed and ready. I'd sit with her and feed her, watching her eyes in the glow of the nightlight.

I was sleep deprived, but I got used to it. More than that, I looked forward to those quiet moments with only her and me awake when the rest of the world seemed to be asleep. It almost saddened me the first time she slept through the night.

My Emma. My Sunshine.

I lean forward and put my face in my hands. I feel like crying but I don't. I know tonight is the last time I'll see my little girl, and part of me is already hard at work, putting stones back in place in my tower.

My phone buzzes in my purse, and I pull it free to check the screen. It's Detective Brewster, and . . . I don't think so. I slide it back into my purse while it continues to ring and then finally goes quiet again.

I can't be here.

I stand, pick up my purse, and hear a short buzz from my phone. As I walk back to my car, I listen to the voicemail.

"Miss Jacobsen, this is Detective Brewster. I'd really like to talk with you, ask you a few questions about Carl Stenson. As I understand it, you're on . . . vacation from work. Hope you're still in town. It'd be great to see you in person."

I can't be here, and there's only one place I can think of that no one would come looking for me. A shack in the middle of nowhere.

I've driven almost a third of the way to Chuy's Fix-It-Up Shop when I realize I don't have the key.

I pull my car over, five houses down from mine, and observe for a moment. I don't see anything that looks like an unmarked cop car, and I pull away from the curb and straight into my driveway, get out, and leave the driver's side door open.

Just as I reach my front porch, I hear hurried footsteps coming toward me, and my stomach drops.

There's a team of police with bulletproof vests and machine guns closing in on me, charging the front of my house, ready to slam me to the ground and cuff me.

"Caroline? Caroline, are you okay?"

My hand still on the porch railing, I turn and see no one there but Darren. He's wearing an argyle sweater vest of browns and pinks, and the only thing more concerning than that fashion statement is Darren's worried expression.

"I'm good, Darren, I just—"

"The cops were here earlier, asking for you."

Fuck. That's more serious than I thought. I definitely can't be here.

"What did you say?"

"I told them I hadn't seen you today. Is that . . . " He flicks his tongue out over his lips and glances around, scanning the street. He lowers his voice when he continues. "Is that what I should've said? Would it be better if I'd told them—"

"It's okay, Darren, I'm—"

"If they come back, I can tell them I saw you or that we had lunch to—"

"Darren—"

"—gether. I'd do that for you. It's a little white lie, but—"

"Darren, I—"

"I'd do that. It's not like I'm robbing a bank or—"

"Darren, shut up!"

He recoils as if I've slapped him, and I immediately feel bad about it, but as they say, it is what it is.

"I'm sorry, Darren. It's okay. You tell them the truth, it's okay."

"But if it's better to tell them I saw you, I—"

"Tell them what you want, Darren. Whatever you want."

I turn and leave him in my driveway, charge into my house and run up the stairs to my bedroom. My jeans are in the clothes basket by my bed and I fish around in my pockets, grab the key, and hurry back outside. Darren's still standing in the driveway, and I wonder, with how he's dressed, if he's going house to house today, spreading the holy word about the good book.

He opens his mouth to say something as I rush past him and get into my car. "Great cookies, by the way! Really good!" I close the door, throw the car in reverse, and drive away as fast as I can.

<hr>

I park farther from the road than I usually do, down and to the left, right behind the rear of the building. It's not much cover, but it's something.

My car is an archaeological dig of memories with Emma. In the passenger side floorboard, I see one of those mini-boxes of Crayons, the kind they hand out at diners for kids to color with while you wait for your meal.

In my center console, I see a wrapper for a candy jewel ring, and when I turn around to look at her booster seat, I see a pink butterfly barrette resting there. An empty juice box, straw still in it, sits against the cushion, somehow still upright after all this time.

I consider getting out and walking around, looking through the windows of the burned farmhouse, but instead, I adjust my seat, listen to the big quiet nothing out here, and fall asleep.

<hr>

I'm dreaming, and it's one of those dreams where you kind of know it, but not really, not enough to do anything about it. I'm on my knees, in front of my house, wearing gardening gloves and using a hand spade to dig a hole. Beside me is a black plastic tray of marigolds in various shades of orange and yellow. I select one, massage the ball of dirt the plant clings to before setting it in the hole I've made, and then scoop soil up close to the stem.

"Is it time to water, Mommy?"

I turn and Emma's there, wearing her pretty black dress. She holds a green watering can in front of her, and I nod and smile.

"I'll take a drink first, and then the flowers."

Emma grabs the plastic with both hands and tilts it to her mouth. I want to tell her not to, but it's too late and she drinks heavily from the container. She smiles as she lowers the can, and wipes her mouth with her forearm.

That's when I see the water, leaking from her body, and when I look at her face again, it's a mottled gray color of death, of pain.

I fall backward in the grass and Emma steps forward, ignoring the streams of water coming from the stab wounds on her torso. She tilts the watering can over the marigold and I watch a stream of blood falling down, down, down over the bloom and the leaves, and the freshly turned earth drinks it up.

———

It's dark outside, and the crickets have come to life, filling the night with their love songs. My heart lurches in my chest and I scramble for my phone to check the time, reaching for it with one hand as I pull the latch to open my car door with the other.

11:57 PM

I run from the car, pull the key from my pocket, and using my phone's flashlight, I slide it home into the lock.

The smell hits me as I rush inside, the dust and neglect, the abandonment of it all, and I run down the aisle between the shelves, dodging the parts scattered on the floor. The end of the *Star-Spangled Banner* plays as I dive through the curtain of beads and drop to my knees in front of the television set.

I sit with my Emma, and because I'm not sure what else to do, I try to make her laugh, soothe her, calm her, because I have no idea what happens after the TV fades to black tonight.

But right now, I'm here.

Right now, I'm here and I'm her mother, and she's my daughter, and I'm doing what mothers are supposed to do—make their children better.

And I'm telling Emma, for the countless time, about the day we went to the beach, and a seagull bombed me. I'm getting close to the actual bird pooping part of the story.

She's been putting on a brave face, and I think she knows I'm upset and lost inside, but Emma's not showing it. She's been going along with me on storytelling and giggles.

But not now.

"Mommy?"

"What, baby?"

Emma's eyes widen, and her lips part slightly. When she talks, it's in a scared whisper.

"The Birdman is here."

I turn slowly, toward the bead curtain. The glow of the TV

screen barely reaches the door frame to the rear of the building, but my eyes have adjusted to the dim interior.

Feet scuff against the gritty floor. Something reaches through the curtain of beads and sweeps them aside so the rest of the figure can step through.

The beads rattle together as it stands there, a hooded cloak pulled down over its face.

I hear it breathe.

A hand reaches up and adjusts the hood, pulls it away, and I can see a leering grin. "Been wondering where you've been going to every night."

"Leave my Mommy alone!" Emma screams from the TV, and, my motherly instincts still intact, I snap my head toward her, realizing my mistake way too late as heavy footsteps charge toward me.

The side of my head detonates and the room fills with fireworks as I fall. Smell of mold and plaster dust fills my nostrils and the couch cushion material feels rough, like worn burlap, against my cheek. My mind swirls and I hear a high-pitched ringing in my ears. There's movement behind me, but I can't lift my head to see.

"There's a sweet little angel."

I blink, still seeing starbursts, and force my head to move with sheer will.

Darren stands there, a hand on his knee, leaning toward the TV.

Emma's face, my god, her face, twisting up with fear. Was that how she looked before she died?

That thought makes my entire body stiffen, and I grab the revolver from my purse, twist my arm around toward Darren, and pull the trigger. It's harder to pull than I thought, and for a moment, I think I'm not going to be able to, but my finger squeezes tightly.

And the hammer clicks dry.

Darren's other hand holds a length of two by four, and he rears back and swings toward me. I raise my arm to defend my head, but his aim is much lower. My breath leaves my lungs in a massive, violent rush, and I actually feel my ribs break—the bones snapping like cold carrots.

Darren kneels in front of me, and I see the side of his face in the glow of the TV.

He smells sickly sweet, of melted sugar and cinnamon. "I must apologize for my curiosity, following you out here, and I suppose . . . well . . . "

Darren's face changes to his sitcom Dad smile. "There's no chance for us now, but I guess it needed to be like this, right? Even if I hadn't come out here tonight, we'd still be over, when you went to the cops, and I can't have that."

He shakes his head slightly. "I still have work to do."

My ribs are shards of fluorescent light bulbs, they are crushed gravel and lengths of hot barbed wire.

Darren turns his head toward the TV and chuckles lightly. "Birdman." He pulls down the neckline of his hoodie, and in the dim light I see his necklace, a gold silhouette of a dove.

"Gift from my mother, long ago." He lets the fabric back in place. "I know you're wondering why Emma? Why Katie and the others? They're so innocent. Free of sin. Sweet little doves. I know I shouldn't be, but I'm . . . " Darren glances toward the ceiling and then back to me. "I covet, and I envy their purity . . . Sweet. So, so sweet."

"You son of—"

"Sometimes, I used to watch her sleep at night. Through her window at first, but that wasn't enough, so I, I just had to get closer, you know? Put my hand against her angelic little face."

Darren watches Emma on the TV, and I see the terror in her eyes.

"I'll . . . fucking . . . " My voice is wind through a hole in a paper bag. The rustling of dry leaves.

"*Shhhh. Shhh* now. I couldn't let them be corrupted. No." He shakes his head side to side with his bottom lip stuck out like a headstrong toddler. "Couldn't let the world turn them into . . . something else, something defiled and impure."

I'm still holding the pistol at my side, behind my right leg, and I use my thumb to ease the hammer back. The clicking noise is loud, too loud, and before I can summon the strength to aim it at Darren's face, he grabs my wrist, squeezes and twists, and my fingers spring open like a coin-operated claw machine. The revolver falls to the floor, and Darren gives my wrist one more vicious squeeze before he slings it away from him.

When he lifts the gun, he turns it one way and then the other as I first did, his gaze on the way the light plays over the steel.

I cough and it feels like I've been hit with a sledgehammer in my chest. My teeth clench and my eyes squeeze shut. My hands and fingers stiffen against the floor and touch something there.

Darren inhales and exhales slowly.

"Don't hurt my mommy."

He turns to Emma and smiles. "She won't feel a thing." He rests one knee on the floor to steady himself, and then raises the gun in his hand, aiming toward my head. "Like I said, I have so much work left to do."

With every last shred of strength, I tighten my right hand and shove it straight toward Darren's face. There is a massive explosion as the pistol fires, and I watch Darren try and stumble away. I pull back and lunge toward him, ignoring the eruptions of pain along my side

He falls to both knees, and I push the screwdriver deeper into his eye socket. Darren's arms twitch and then shake as if he's having a fit, and then he falls hard against the floor. In the light of the TV screen, I see the liquid flowing down his face.

There is nothing but static on the screen as I slump backward.

"Sun—" I hiss in breath through the pain. "Sunshine? It's okay . . . it's okay, baby."

"Is the Birdman gone, Mommy?"

Emma's face swirls back into form. "He's gone, baby. He . . . he won't be back. You can . . . you can rest now. It's okay."

"Will you lay here with me and Bobo, Mommy?"

"Yes, baby." I smile through the agony inside me.

I want to lay down and curl up, but I don't dare try. The broken parts of my ribs grind against each other with the slightest breath. I raise my left hand, gently touch my ribs, and then pull it away quickly. My fingertips are wet.

On the floor beside the coffee table, I see the length of wood Darren used on me. A sun-bleached two by four, almost silver in the dim, and the end closest to me has several twists of nails protruding from the wood like seedlings reaching for the sun.

I ease my jacket away and see the punctures in my side, the giant hibiscus-shape, blood as dark as obsidian in the light.

"Mommy?"

"I'm here, baby. You just . . . close your eyes."

I put my jacket back in place, and rest my bloody hand on the floor. On TV, Emma's face is at peace. Her eyes are closed and Bobo is hugged up close to her.

"You are my Sunshine, my only . . . Sunshine." At first, I was breathing shallow on purpose, but now, now I'm breathing shallow because it's all my body will allow.

"You make me . . . ha . . . happy, when skies are gray."

Emma's breath deepens, slows as she begins to drift.

"You'll never . . . know, dear, how much . . . I . . . "

I can't finish the last of the song. I'm incapable of it, but that's okay. Emma's eyes are closed and I hear her soft, gentle breathing. I feel a cold breeze rise up around me, but it's comforting. The waist of my jeans is soaked with blood. I want so badly to cough, but I grit my teeth and stifle it.

It's been four months and one week since I kissed you and held you close and told you how much I love you.

But I will soon, Sunshine.

I will soon.

SUET

—✦—

JOHN BODEN

*" . . . the mud and the roots
know your name."*
—Pablo Neruda

PROLOGUE

F OR CORBIN WORTHY, sleep was a reckless thing. It often swerved from the road, into the forest of thoughts that never stilled. His body feigned rest; his eyelids fluttered. Ever since he climbed into adulthood all those years ago, putting it on like the ill-fitting suit that so many wear with strut and pretense of comfort, it had been like this. He conjured up voices and dialogue from years past, from people long dead, playing them in the speakers of his mind to soothe, calm and lull him until, eventually the pacing sleep—that wickedly unrestful thing—slowed its circles and finally fell still.

"A poet might say that time is a stitch that dangles, that seduces, that begs to be gripped between fingers or teeth and pulled to delicious agony. Awakening wounds and courting blood, opening eyes and closing hearts. A bad barter or a lip in need of splitting. That's all time is. Best dust off your knuckles, kiddo.'Things go on as they're meant to, they go on until they stop or change into something else. Takes very little: a tragedy, a miracle, a wish or a worry . . . transformation is the oldest talent. Time and transformation and balance: that's the true Trinity,boy. Time sits at the right hand and change squats on the left, Balance is straight and tall in the throne, because when that teeter-totter dance of the scales gets to one side more than the other, that's when things go pear-shaped. Delicate balance is what separates . . . time and transformation have themselves a good ol' hootenanny, world be damned. And for that matter, damn you, too."

The old man's voice was still rasping through his mind when Corbin sat on the edge of the rumpled bed, knuckling sleep from his bleary eyes. His fingers were wet, as if he'd been crying in his slumber. Those recollected sermons and conversations usually assuaged his fitfulness. This particular one, for one reason or another, had the opposite effect. He frowned, trying to place that talk, the precise circumstances around the old man saying such things to him.

When he was a boy staying at the farm, the environment was much quieter than he was used to, even in his small town. There was a deeper quiet marred only by cricket song, whispering breezes, and peeping frogs when it was the season for them. The old man would read to him until Corbin's eyes began to droop, then he would sit and just talk until well after Corbin had begun to snore. Maybe this talk was from one of those times, and Corbin had no real memory of it because it had seeped into his subconscious, lodging like a sliver of bone in the throat.

He sighed and shook his head, then stood, looking into the darkness of the far end of the bedroom, where he knew a window lived, staring hard to see into the woods beyond the edge of his yard. Night and shadow wove tightly. All he saw were occasional streaks of white flitting through, like watching grainy film stock. He felt his heart beating in his chest, just a little bit faster than usual. He drew the curtains closed.

1.

Gray, gloomy morning. A wind-swept Tuesday. Corbin was at the end of the counter, sitting where he usually did on the stool nearest the wall, propping his weary self against its cool plaster while he waited for his breakfast. He stared at the smoke curling from the end of a bent cigarette butt, dying in the ashtray.

"God bless small towns, black lungs and the corners where the light of the law don't reach sometimes."

His father's voice mumbled behind his eyes, woodgrain deep and steeped in nicotine and coffee. Corbin picked up the squashed pack of smokes from the worn Formica and shook it until one poked its head out. He lipped and lit it in a motion borne of decades of rehearsal. The smoke filled his barrel chest, igniting all the bulbs in his lungs. It trickled from his nose in a faint fog.

Cammy set the plate before him. "Here's your mess, Hun." Her smile was bright, ringed by red lips.

"Thank you."

Corbin nodded and sucked one more time on his smoke before he dropped it into the untouched glass of water beside his coffee cup. He cleared his throat and pulled himself upright and forward.

"Manners, boy, manners. God dammit, belly up to the table and sit straight."

This was followed by an imaginary tap to the back of his head. Corbin smiled at the memory of his great grandma's admonishments. She never cussed to that degree, but the voice in his head this time was hers nonetheless. He picked up a fork and went to work on his plate of eggs, peppers and ham, all fried together, surrounded by triangles of rye toast. He tried not to watch the haggard man in the mirror matching his moves and gluttony. He finished the food in less than twelve minutes—far from a personal best.

"So, what brings you in for breakfast on a Tuesday, Cor? You ain't usually in for nothin' but a burger or maybe a Reuben other than Monday nights. You change shifts again?"

Cammy leaned against the back counter, where the coffee maker burbled and glupped. Through the open window above her shoulders, the heads of the cook staff whizzed by like strange creatures. Metal clanged and dishes clinked.

"Kinda." The sound of his own voice surprised him. It felt like weeks since he'd had it out of the box, let it jump in the light and air. His tongue might ache just from the effort.

Cammy raised an eyebrow and pulled a piece of hard candy from her apron pocket. "I'm quitting smokes," she said. "Been doing real good too, but you're makin' me want one." The cellophane crinkled as she undressed the mint and tossed it on her tongue.

"I left," Corbin tacked on, matter-of-factly.

"Like for good left? As in quit? Oh, Corbin. What happened?" Her eyebrows high in surprise, Cammy came around and took the empty seat beside him. He gritted his teeth at the thought of what he knew was coming next, and continued as it did: the girl placed her bony hand on his arm, electric blanket-warm.

"I had to. I was close to losing it."

"Losing what? Your motivation? Honey, we all do that. Every job is a leech at times. A wage ain't payment for a job you do, it's a petty barter for your soul. My nan used to say that. I get it." She paused, her lips disappearing into her small mouth. "You do good work there, though. Sometimes there's payment and labor that isn't measured in money and sweat."

The end of her statement caused a hitch in his attentiveness, feeling in some way like a tiny filament with a barbed hook had caught in his back brain and pulled. Almost a memory.

"It was taking a toll, Cammy. I was feeling like a beach—how the ocean eats it slowly and daily, in a way that you can't notice outright. Well, I was starting to notice. I tried to keep at it. I love them old folks. I like being a help to them. I like making it easier for them. Holding the door."

"I don't care if you're a religious person or whatever, but Corbin, you were called to that job. You're a big man with a bigger heart. Big enough to hold all that hurt you hoard, and still have love for the world. You're kind and gentle, and those old folks know it. They need that."

"I hear that shit all the time. You'd think a calling would feel like it, ya know? It'd feel good, right?" He never looked her in the eye as he spoke, but instead concentrated on the corpse of his cigarette floating in the glass by his plate.

"I can imagine it's hard, but the old folks love you. They actually ask for rooms in your hall. My maw-maw thought you were the best. Talked like you was one of her own when she was near the end, she'd grown so fond of you. And Mr Clark, Ol' Neff Harper and old Miss Potts . . . for them and the others you've helped, you were an offering from careful gods."

The invisible test line pulled again, the almost memory stretching like old rubber, cracking a little.

"Stop. I mean. Thank you. And yeah, I know, but can you really imagine what it's like? It's hard enough to be a nurse or caregiver in an old folk's home. All day lifting people with one arm because time has picked them to bones. Or introducing yourself every time you dole out meds because they can't retain a memory for more than a few hours or minutes at a time. That shit is brutal anyway. But anymore, I'm spoon-feeding people who I knew back when I was at friends' houses as a kid. Their parents. I'm doing that job in a facility just outside of my hometown. Almost everyone who comes through the goddamn door—be they wheeled in or hobbling behind a cane or walker—they're someone I know. They aren't patients or names on file tabs hidden in cold cabinets. They aren't just letters typed on some plastic bracelet. It's never 'the woman in room twelve', or 'the old geezer in twenty'. For me, it's always Mrs Creswell who taught me in third grade. It's Mr Wible, who used to live on the corner across from the post office and would tell me stories about when he was a young man in the Navy. It's watching Alzheimer's swallow the mind of my high school principal in greedy little gulps."

Corbin went silent. His eyes grew moist and his cheeks flushed. He sighed before speaking again, fighting to keep his voice even and calm. "It was my own fucking grandmother . . . worn down to a husk but smiling as best she could when I went in, because she didn't want her grandson to know how bad it hurt." He stopped short. His voice was dry and brittle. He drew a breath and wiped his eyes with the back of his hand and looked around. No one was watching. "Every wrinkled face becomes a brick in the wall of my tomb. You know, like in that Poe story. But I feel . . . felt . . . like both the dude behind the wall going up and the bastard building it."

He stopped speaking, his head was light and swirling inside. He hadn't voiced his thoughts for a long time. It felt alien. He swung a gaze to Cammy. Her eyes were sad and welling with wetness. Her hand stayed on his arm. The skin beneath it felt about to sizzle.

"Oh honey. I'm sorry. I never stopped to think."

"Don't be. It's fine. I fell into that line of work. All of this mess I call my life is mine. It's a little bit of everything that's brought me down to this. I gathered the fixins, and I made the meal for myself. I ate it for a long, long time. But now, after too long, I decided it was time to push my fat ass away from the table and make some changes."

He leaned forward enough to shimmy his wallet free, took some bills from it and laid them on the counter. He drained the last of the cold coffee from his cup and stood to leave.

Cammy stood with him, her hand still on his arm. "Corbin, I know there's a reward for you out there for all you've done. I know it feels like you've been pissing in a waterfall, but I know in my heart there's a plan with you in it."

The aged tether line snapped with a *sproing*, and the sketch of a memory pulled free from the mire in his head. It was dark and nearly impossible to read. He felt his forehead creasing with the effort.

"Cor, are you gonna be alright?"

He saw sincere concern in her eyes. He managed a tiny smile that he knew was probably mostly hidden beneath his unruly beard.

"As alright as any of us, I suppose." He patted her hand with his meatier paw, and exited the diner. The cowbell on the nail clanged his departure.

Cammy punched some buttons on the register and fed it Corbin's money. The worry lines on her forehead were slow to fade away.

2.

He spent the entire day just walking around town. The library. The pizza shop for late lunch. The graveyard behind the Methodist Church. He meandered around the mile-long stretch of life as he'd always known it. His small town. There were four messages on the machine by the time Corbin got home that evening. He stood in the dim corner of the small living room and watched the red light blink twenty-seven times before he thumbed the playback button.

"Corbin. This is Darla. I tried your cell but you don't have voicemail set up or nothin'. Tammy from the morning crew said you never came back from your break at five. Thought maybe you walked down the street for smokes, but after an hour figured not. She said you seemed off and I wanted to reach out and make sure you weren't sick or anything. Give me a call back please when you get this. Uh, thanks."

Two similar messages followed, each growing in agitation dressed as urgency. The final message was just a muffled voice mumbling and a click. He rewound the last one and listened to it a few more times. *"Gaum,"* it sounded like it said.

The low voice almost tripped some recollection in him, but sounded so far away he couldn't get around it tight enough. He picked up the phone and listened to the drone of the dial tone before he pushed down the cradle button and laid the receiver on the counter. He went to the far side of the room and plopped down in the recliner. The spread of light from the dining room didn't quite make the journey to where he sat, leaving him to rub shoulders with shadows. The digital clock on top of the television read almost eight-thirty. The first dozen hours of rogue behavior didn't feel that different. He put his head back against the cushion, and despite the growl of thunder outside, fell asleep within minutes.

3.

It was Friday afternoon when the letter arrived. Since walking away from the home three days prior, Corbin had done nothing but sleep off and on. He figured the twenty-plus years of swing shifts and doubles had left him sufficiently worn down, and he needed the rest.

He was standing in the kitchen drinking milk from the carton when he heard the mailbox lid clank as it dropped back in place. He shuffled to the door and opened it, shirtless and in boxers, and reached out into the metal receptacle. He made his way back to his chair and sat down. He fanned the five envelopes out on the coffee table like the worst hand of cards. Electric bill, Sewer. Heating and Cable. He dragged the fifth and final one away from the others, and looked at the plain writing on the front. No sender address, just his, written in stark, slightly-tilting print.

The wild card, he thought, and used a too-long thumbnail to tear it open. He pulled out the letter.

Dear Mr Worthy . . . regret to inform you of the passing of your great grandfather, Silas Worthy . . . recent illness . . . you are the sole remaining family . . . unable to contact you by phone . . . in lieu of will he left this letter as well as specific instructions on our end, which we have carried out so far and will follow through. We are terribly sorry for your loss.

No signature. No letterhead. Just a plain piece of stationary. Odd.

Corbin let the paper fall to the table, and stared at it. Being a layman, even the words and phrases he understood seemed to scurry like ants. He sighed and felt tears threatening. Pap was gone. He picked up the smaller envelope, one that had been nesting in the other. Tore the left side off and slid the thin sheet of grayish tablet paper free. His eyes teared up as soon as he saw the stilted chicken scratch of his Pap's hand. He drew a breath and began to read the single paragraph the letter bore.

Corbin boy,

If you're reading this, I'm gone. And you are where you are, which is how I always was glad for it to be. I wanted you to know that my lack of staying close wasn't nothin' to do with you. I love you. Always have. Nothing is more treasure in this old heart of mine than watching you grow into the man you are, two weeks of summer and a few weekends a year . . . I'm proud of you. Of what you're doing. I never was good at getting to the point. Evy told me that often. The house is to be sold, and all the contents. There is nothing for you there, trust me. Nothing of want. I wanted to let you know that so you wouldn't feel any slight. The valley ain't for you. You got your own thing going. The lawyer will take care of everything. All you need to do is send him the key you have from when your Gramma was ill, and you came to stay. I'm sorry, boy, that I didn't let you know I was sick. That I didn't ever discuss things with you. There was so much to say and I just didn't. Wouldn't. And I think we got away with it . . .

"Got away with it? *Aw* . . . " Corbin frowned. He imagined the old man tottering about the big farmhouse alone, in the obvious throes of early dementia of some sort, while Corbin just worked and slept. His heart hurt: a sharp pinch of regret and grief he was quite familiar with. He put the letter on top of the others and sat back.

His mind played back those late summer days of running the fields of the farm. Bare feet on muddy soil. Watching the droning silhouette of his pap on the tractor against the orange of the setting sun. He could still smell all the smells of those days. The hay. The cow shit. The thick scent of moist earth turned. The sweet tang of icy water from the pump well. The ditch along the upper pasture where his pap disposed of dead things, and neighbors dumped their trash. The smell of the river when it grew emaciated by the summer heat. He could still see the big yellow farmhouse with its dark green trim. The old beagle sleeping on the concrete porch. The trees that surrounded the big yard, tallow draped over their branches.

"Pap, what is that stuff hanging up there on them branches?"

"That's just suet."

"What's that? Looks like slimy ghosts?"

"Suet . . . tallow."

"What's tallow?"

"When we butcher, we try not to waste nothin'. Even when we ain't butcherin', in all we do we try not to waste. We cut the fat away in strips. The harder fat is called suet or tallow. String it up and sling it in the trees, over the branches for the birds, beetles and things to eat."

"What things besides birds?"

"Good for them," the old man continued, ignoring the boy's question. "Shines the feathers, makes the shells of their eggs harder and makes 'em sing prettier. Always a way to repay, boy."

"Things," little Corbin muttered as he trapsed ahead of his pap, in the direction of the well pump.

"C'mon now, let's wash up for supper."

"What'd Gramma make? I hope it's sugar ham and mashed potatoes."

"I don't know, but I'm hungry enough to eat it. Let's git goin'. Hit the handle."

Corbin snapped back from his memories. Now Pap was dead, even though it had been nearly a decade since he'd last seen him, since right after Gramma had passed away. This news had gashed into him like claws, deep and painful. He drew a heavy breath and allowed himself to cry.

For his great grandpa and gramma, no longer living,

For the old folks, the many gone and those no longer cared for but cared about.

For the large chunk of his life that was behind him.

For the uncertainty of what was ahead.

For himself and the whole damn world, in anger and solidarity, Amen.

Corbin Worthy wept.

4.

Narcolepsy had kept him from getting a driver's license, so he called on his oldest pal, Mike, to give him a ride out to the farm and then return for him the following weekend. He had somewhat grown out of the condition that made him fall asleep almost upon sitting down or standing still, but it was still a major hindrance when it came to travel. As soon as the car or truck started moving, within minutes, his eyelids would be at half-mast, and then he'd be down for the count for nearly the entirety of the drive.

Corbin threw another pair of jeans into the old vinyl suitcase and closed it. He looked at the bed and considered taking one of his own pillows, but decided to make do with what was at the farm. He carried the case to the living room and dropped it beside the front door, next to another smaller case and a backpack stuffed so full it looked like a tick about to pop. He sat on the sofa and looked at the clock. Mike had said four sharp. Ten minutes to go. Corbin grabbed the remote and pushed the button, turning on the TV. The volume was loud, exploding into the silence that had cradled the room. Corbin turned it down and flipped through the channels, eventually stopping on an episode of *Columbo*.

By the time Johnny Cash, a big cast on his leg, came limping into the studio to chat with the rumpled detective, Corbin felt his eyes growing heavy. He sat up straighter and opened his eyes as wide as possible, keeping them open without blinking until the sting became unbearable. The man in black was playing a gospel song for Columbo. Corbin was about to go open the door and let the fresh air smack him awake when he heard the shrill beep of Mike's car horn. He sighed and turned off the set. With the backpack slung over his shoulder and a case in each hand, he shambled out onto the porch and then down the small hill to the driveway.

"Hey buddy, you going to move the fuck in?" Mike smiled, chiding his friend.

Corbin smiled back, but didn't say anything until after he'd thrown the luggage into the back seat.

"I'll be there for a few days, alone. One suitcase is clothes and stuff, the other is some magazines and movies for evenings. The pack is my heavier coat—it gets cold out there at night, and I don't know the state of the furnace or anything. I just wanna look through things. Find a few keepsakes before the bank sells it all."

"You sure you don't want me to bunk off and stay to help? It could be like camping out," Mike raised his eyebrows. That damn smile again.

"No. Thanks. It shouldn't be too bad. Pap got rid of a lot after Gramma passed. Even though I'm sad about Pap being gone . . . I'm using this alone time as a reset for me. I've had a lot on my mind since I quit the home, even before that, and I think the solitude and work will help me sort myself out a bit. Find my purpose, as they say. I hope."

"Keep your phone charged and text me if you need anything. If anything happens or if you get lonely, promise. I mean it."

"You'll make some lucky fella a wonderful wife one day," Corbin joked, patting his friend's cheek.

"God, I hope so."

They laughed and Mike slowly backed into the street, brakes squeaking slightly, and then they were off.

5.

"Looks just like I remember."

Mike sat sideways in the driver's seat, feet on the ground, hunched forward and his hands crammed in his jacket pockets. When he spoke, small curls of steam blossomed from his lips. The sun was retreating behind the rise, and shadows were beginning to sprout around them. It was only the end of October, but the nights were definitely getting colder.

"Yeah, Pap and Gramma weren't much for changing things that didn't need it. Shit, I'm a few months from forty and this house has been this goldy yellow all my life. And according to photographic evidence and stories from Mom, all of hers as well." Corbin blew smoke into the air and watched the cloud disappear into the withering daylight.

"Okay, let's get you settled so this young man can get home and to bed. I've got work tomorrow."

"'Young man'? Mike, we've been friends since second grade and I'm just about forty."

Mike responded with another smile. He had thousands, it seemed.

Corbin grabbed the suitcases from the backseat and Mike took the bulging pack, and together they clomped down the walk to the house. The porch light burning confirmed that the power was thankfully on, as the lawyer's letter had assured him it would be. The door opened into the kitchen, which was exactly as it had always been. The east wall was flanked by a long counter that cut to a large basin sink with wall-mounted cabinets running the upper length. The countertop section right inside the door always acted as his pap's desk, and was full of the old man's accumulated hodge-podge. Tools and pencils. Old newspapers and puzzle magazines. Worn western paperbacks and half-empty pouches of chewing tobacco. Bills, invoices and scraps of paper with his scrawled numbers and notations tattooed on them. Corbin felt a small smile growing. It was like he'd traveled back through time. Almost.

"Okay. I'll stick around while you go make sure the furnace is working. I'm not leaving you to freeze, but I'm also not going down in that cellar. I've seen that movie. I hear a chainsaw, I'm gone." Mike pulled out a chair from the table and dropped himself into it. He started reading one of the old tabloids from a pile stacked beside the large glass dish that probably held bread or rolls during meals. It was empty now.

Corbin stomped down the cellar steps. He pulled the chain to the bare bulb that dangled from a cord above the ancient washing machine. A plump spider retreated up a web connecting ceiling to the pull cord. The single bulb illuminated the end of the basement wall, and was as terrifying now as it had been when he was ten. Cement, cobwebs, the smell of damp wood and mud. Old wooden shelves full of faded paint cans and tins of oil. Rags so stiff with time and dried who-knows-what that they resembled petrified creatures. Jars of preserved vegetables or fruits, now just cloudy orange and yellow jewels in a basement crypt crown. The furnace was small but efficient, and a piece of paper was taped to the side. It was a schedule card that noted the last servicing of the unit, dated two months earlier, so all ought to be in working order. Corbin flipped the switch and listened as the furnace roared to life. He hunkered there until he heard the gurgling that told him the water was heating for the radiators. Knees popping, he rose and mounted the steps to the kitchen where his friend waited. He left the light on.

6.

"I thought you were in a hurry to get home to bed?" Corbin parked himself in the chair at the end of the table.

Mike kept reading, nodding as he held up a finger. He bobbed his head faster, indicating he was about done, and then closed the tabloid and put it back on the stack. "Oh, how I've missed Bat Boy and the furry adventures of Bigfoot," Mike beamed.

"The shit papers were Gramma's, all she read was them and Ellery Queen. Pap read westerns and the Farmers Almanac, that's all . . . Once in a blue moon he'd read the newspaper, but he mostly had no time for that nonsense."

"He was always working when I was here with you guys. I think it was my third time visiting with you when I first actually saw him, like up close."

"He'd be out in the field at sunup. If the weather was cooperative he'd not set foot back in the house until the sun limped off. He'd take a couple of butter and tomato sandwiches with him in a bag to eat on the tractor. He was a work beast." Corbin stared out the large window behind the table, out on the front yard. The large oak still stood by the shed and old outhouse, near the end of the driveway. He could just make out its branches against a darkening sky. He saw Mike's car sitting in the rapidly diminishing light. He stood and patted his friend on the shoulder. "Mike, thanks for bringing me out. You better get on the road if you wanna get home and to bed before it gets too late."

"Yeah, you're right. I'll see you in a few days. You just call me if you need me before."

Corbin hugged the smaller man and walked him to the end of the walk. "You got it."

"I fucking mean it. I'll worry about you out here in Aintree by yourself." Mike frowned to emphasize his seriousness as he got into the car.

"This river don't go there," Corbin dead-panned in a horrible drawl, and they both laughed until Corbin spoke again. "Watch for deer, especially when you get near the bridge, where the old Yocum road splits."

"Sure will. See ya, Hoss." Mike put the car in gear, and the crunching stones sang of his exit. Corbin waited until the taillights disappeared around the bend before he shuffled back to the house.

7.

Corbin stared at the ancient set with its dusty rabbit ears on top. He sighed and dropped the top of the small suitcase full of DVDs closed. He wasn't sure why he had assumed they'd have a player. There wasn't even a VCR. Just the old black & white set sitting on the same dusty table where it had lived for as long as he could remember. He flipped the switch and watched as a small dot appeared in the center of the screen. Through the speaker came a high-pitched whine, almost a whistle. The dot grew slowly, and within a few minutes the screen was filled with a washed-out picture. Barely any definition, and the audio sounded like it was coming from under a pillow, but it was better than nothing. Corbin sat on the edge of Gramma's recliner and watched as Jack Lord chased a young Hawaiian across a beach, his hair not moving.

"I didn't even know this show was still on," Corbin mumbled.

After ten minutes, he turned it off. The poor picture and the smell of hot metal that was starting to emanate from the set were both deciding factors. He stood and walked across to the staircase to the second floor. He gazed into the darkness above and saw the pale rectangles of the doors. Three of them. All closed with clothesline rope tying the knobs together. Hanging from the approximate middle of the rope was a piece of cardboard with the words DO NOT OPEN—BATS written in large, leaning print. He knew this not from actual sight, but because that was how they had been when last was here. Corbin recalled the ongoing feud between Gramma and the attic bats that eventually led to the old woman's surrender of the second floor of her house to the winged critters.

"Let 'em have it. I got the stove and the TV, they want an old dresser and boxes of outgrown clothes, let 'em have it."

He leaned forward, straining to hear the squeaking from behind the doors. He used to be able to hear them as a child, sometimes sneaking up as far as the seventh step before Gramma would smack her hand on the table and holler.

"Get back down here and into this kitchen, boy!"

His footsteps on the uncarpeted steps echoed about the large rooms. Corbin held his breath and listened to nothing but silence from upstairs.

Maybe the bats are gone and they just didn't want to deal with the damage?

The grumble of his own stomach startled him, and he jumped where he stood. He stilled again and listened for a few more seconds. He could almost make out squeaking, a high-pitched pulse. The toe of his boot clipped something on the edge of the third step from the bottom. He looked down into the shadows, trying to see what it was. He knelt and picked it up. It was a box turtle's shell, placed upside down with a thick yellow candle in the center. Long strands of melted wax held it in place, and around its base were several small stones. Some shined like quartz, some were tan and smooth. Three fish hooks had been pushed into the base of the candle, and tied around each were knots of what looked like hair or animal fur. Corbin grimaced as he sat the weird object back where it was. He wiped his hands on his jeans.

"Probably some folky hocus pocus. Definitely dumpster-bound," he mumbled.

He remembered the mustard poultice his grandma made for him, back when he was a child and had come down with a fever one late summer day—slathering his then-slight chest with a thick yellow salve made of mustard seed and liniment of some sort, the odor all but carving its way into his sinuses. He remembered her halving a large onion, putting the pieces into a white china dish, and sliding it under his bed. The next morning, he awoke devoid of fever and congestion. The only evidence of the ick on his chest was a faint yellow tint to the skin, like a large birthmark. He had called for his grandma, and she came quickly. She'd smiled, and touched his brow with her slender hand.

"That did the trick, hmm?"

When she knelt and slid the dish from under the bed, he was

sure he saw dark, wriggling things in the fetid mush that now filled the vessel. The onion looked as though it had been moldering for weeks.

Corbin shook his head clear of the webs of those memories, and went back into the kitchen to find something to eat. Behind him and above, in one of the unused rooms, the sound of squeaking rose in volume ever so slightly.

8.

He stared at the plate, at the crumbs and bits of crust that littered it. For a sandwich he'd picked up at the Kwik-Mart in town, it was okay. He eyed the clock above the window. The big and little hands were both closing in on the ten. He stood and walked to the counter area by the door, his pap's 'working desk', as he had called it. He pulled the first drawer out and saw no fewer than a thousand buttons and small wooden spools. Coins winked from among the colored plastic and wood. He gently dragged his hand through the contents, decided this was all the drawer held, and sifted out the money, dumping the rest into the trashcan by the stove.

"Sorry, Pap, can't even donate that junk."

His whispered mumbling sounded loud in the empty house. Out on the porch, something scraped the cement, loud—yanking his attention like an errant dog on a lead. He pulled the shade and looked out the window of the door. The large, gray square stone of the porch was well lit by the spotlight above the door. He saw nothing out of place. The old milk box stood by the top step, a bundled hose lay coiled like a snake by the back corner. He was about to reroute his attention back to the task of cleaning out junk drawers when his eyes noticed something new, sitting just in front of the door. A large Mason jar filled with something dark. He knew it hadn't been there when they arrived or he'd have likely tripped on it or knocked it over. He frowned and opened the door to retrieve the mystery item. He held it up in front of the light and saw that the contents were thick and amber in color. He saw bits of white and even what looked to be a dead bee trapped in it.

"It's honey. Must've been from the neighbor. Saw lights and

figured it was family clearing house. I'll go and thank them in the morning."

Corbin nodded, then frowned when he realized he was talking to himself. Again. Back inside, he put the honey on the table and pulled out another drawer. It was empty, save for a desiccated spider and a pair of rusted scissors. The third drawer held rubber bands and a jar of pipe seal that had leaked and fused the squat jar to the old lumber. The fourth held notebooks. Three of them. They were faded and worn and only one had anything written on the cover's subject line. The green one bore the word *Collections*, scribbled in his great-grandfather's hobbled handwriting.

"Your Pap was ambidextrous; he could write with either hand. But when he was a kid, way back, the schools wouldn't allow that, so they made him use the right. They tied his left to the arm of the desk until he no longer tried to use it for things. All that did was make it so that no matter which hand he used, the writing was awful. Mom, my mom—your gram and pap's daughter—was the same way, and they did the same thing to her."

That snippet of conversation with his mother floated to mind when Corbin opened the book, and saw the scrawl that filled the first page. He remembered that day—he'd turned twelve and gotten a birthday card in the mail from Gramma and Pap. Pap signed it and wrote a little message that had had to decipher. Now, after years of working in the home with others of that generation, he could suss out the gist of most elderly handwriting. Corbin sat down and began to look through the notebook.

9.

Silas and Evelyn Worthy were married in 1921. They settled on the farm, which had been built in 1850 by Silas's grandfather, Legam. From the notes in the book, the Worthy clan had always been the tax collectors for the area, and more so in the river valley here. The folks who lived along the banks, in the hills or up the mountain came to them to pay their owings. It also seemed that being a lineage of farmers, the Worthy's delivered fresh produce to folks—and at one time milk and eggs—often for no charge, if times were tough. Which they usually seemed to be.

"Always a way to pay back, boy. A kindness is a gift and a debt is a stone. Both make the world go round but one is much easier to count than the other. Sometimes . . . kindness can also be a debt. And the returning stone is the gift. It's what we think we want or was owed, but really it's just twinkling junk passed off as fine crystal. The eye and the heart, they sort them things."

If he closed his eyes, he could almost see the old man leaning in, conspiratorially delivering those fevered words of wisdom on rich tobacco breath. The voice of his Pap in his ears, he read the words that began halfway down the third page. After that were just uneven columns of last names and numbers. A few of the names had little stars beside them, which according to the crude key at the bottom meant: *'More notes in blue book.'* Corbin fanned through the pages for any mentions of the red notebook and found none. His fingers found the red cover and pulled it from beneath the other two. Corbin opened it and saw the pages filled with his grandfather's errant writing. He flipped through and saw that every page was choked with scrawl. Most pages were topped with a date.

A journal. This one was the old man's journal. Corbin felt the sting of weariness in his eyes and pushed himself away from the table. He looked at the clock once more. Nearing eleven-thirty. He wasn't exactly looking forward to a night on that sofa bed in the living room, but that's what it would be. He ambled into the dark room and turned on the tall lamp by his Pap's empty recliner. Once he had folded down the back of the sofa and arranged the throw pillows to fill the gap down the center, he spread one of the quilts from the chair across it and laid down, pulling the other quilt over himself. He looked at the lamp and the light from the kitchen peeking in from the doorway. Considered getting up to turn them off, but decided not to. He wasn't paying the bill this month.

He closed his eyes, and sleep clobbered him.

10.

"Every house has a heart. Every place for that matter. The fields, the woods . . . all that there is. Boy, I have seen some things and been party to deeds both bad and good. I was kind and I've been mean and I can tell you that the words upon my heart will speak for me when my light puffs out. I ain't sure there's a God. I'm not arrogant enough to say there ain't one, either. I spent all my years trying to keep balance in the valley. I've done good for them what needed it, tried to help others. And, to my remorse, I've had hands in darker things a time or two, also to help others. All that I learned was that dark things seldom go as they promise to . . . Just like regular prayers and hopes, but the scales can and will usually balance."

Corbin's eyes slowly opened in the darkness. The room was black as pitch. He craned his neck to confirm that the lights he had left on were no longer burning.

"Must have been a surge and maybe a fuse blew," he grumbled to himself as he stepped into his unlaced boots and shuffled into the kitchen, arms waving before him to navigate the unfamiliar terrain.

He flicked the switch above the stove and the light popped on. Bright as summer. He saw his plate from earlier was clean, but still sitting where he had left it. The jar of honey sat beside it, lid off and a spoon jutting from the mouth like a limb. He turned and stepped back into the living room where he flicked the switch for the standing lamp by the recliner. It gave light as well. Corbin frowned and went back in the kitchen. He put the lid back on the honey and put it in the fridge.

Maybe I opened it and had a taste while I was looking at the notebooks, and forgot?

After a trip to the bathroom, he went into the living room where he laid down on the sofa, again. He began to think about what he was going to do when he was done here and returned to his apartment. He needed to find a job. He didn't want to go back to the old folk's home. Was anyone going to hire an out-of-shape dude knocking on middle age's door?

Maybe you waited too long to jump, Son . . .

The voice of his father spoke. Corbin responded with a deep breath through his nostrils. His father had always been a stanchion of rough practicality. Rarely held truck in what he called 'idle dreamery'. You work and you earn, in all things. This was a message all the elders in Corbin's life seemed to proselytize, in different clothing and degrees of severity—but the recurring theme was no longer lost on him. He sighed again to the darkness, and had just closed his eyes when he heard the switch click in the kitchen and the light disappeared once more. He sat up and turned to step from the couch. The light by the chair went out.

Old wiring, I guess. I'll sort it out tomorrow.

Corbin laid back down and kept quite still. Eventually his eyes did close. From above, he heard a low, squeaking thrum. He stared into the blackness, trying to see through the floorboards into the bedroom above. Trying to see the bats that were singing. He stared and listened until, eventually, Sleep came again.

In it, he dreamed of the home. Of the old and genial faces of those whose hands he'd held as they drew their last breaths— sometimes peacefully, and other times spastic and filled with terror. He'd caress their small and leathery hands with his thumb and lean in close to the pinched faces. He would sing softly to them, or whisper sweet stories they had told him about during more lucid times. He would cradle them dearly and hold the door for them and watch them go on. As Corbin slept and dreamed, tears wet his hairy cheeks, and his lips curled into a sad smile.

11.

Before he even sat up, Corbin dragged his large hand over his face, smoothing down the beard that was sticking out in a mess so unruly that if he looked down at his nose he could see it. Like some wild bush. He frowned when his fingers felt something sticky the coarse, whiskery hair. He held out his hand and looked at the residue that marred his fingers. He lifted his hand to his nose and inhaled. It was honey. He sat up and shuffled to the kitchen where he saw the jar sitting on the table. Empty. The inside was slick with the remnants of golden sludge. Beside the jar, on his plate from the previous night, was a spoon. Licked clean.

Corbin cocked his head. Narcolepsy had dogged his heels his whole life, but he had never walked in his sleep. Ever. Let alone sleep-eat a whole jar of fucking honey. He picked up the jar and dropped it in the trash can, before stomping to the bathroom to wash his face and get to work. He didn't have the time or mental strength to think about the honey incident. He stared at himself as he brushed his teeth, at the puffy, bruise-toned rings beneath his eyes. He spat into the sink and noted a smear of red among the blueish foam. He smiled in the mirror, lips back and teeth exposed. He watched the small dots of blood appear at the edges, where teeth sprouted from angry gums, and he frowned once more. He looked in the cabinet for floss and found nothing but an old tube of denture adhesive and a jar of black salve. He sighed and closed the door.

Corbin went back to the living room. He considered changing out of yesterday's clothes, and after a short deliberation the vote was unanimous in favor of the T-shirt being granted a second day of wear, along with the jeans and socks and the blue flannel shirt. He went back to the kitchen and cleaned out the cabinets. He placed all the unopened food in bags and then lined them up along the porch for donation. Anything opened or out of date went in the trash. He had asked the lawyer, when he spoke to him about the power, if it was okay to just sort the food stuff for donations— he didn't want it wasted, and the mousy man had said certainly, that was fine. Corbin could separate it, and they'd deal with it when the auctioneer came to assess. It was nearing three o'clock when it occurred to Corbin that he hadn't eaten anything since he got up. The punctuation to that thought being the fact that he wasn't hungry, even then. He turned and saw the notebooks on the table.

A little break couldn't hurt, especially if I'm not gonna eat.

He plopped into the chair, opened the green notebook and started reading the list of names, looking for the ones with the stars after. 'Iness Ichelberger' was the first he came to. He opened the blue notebook and dragged a finger down the columns until he found that man's name. Underlined twice. Then a large block of writing destroyed the column system, as what appeared to be a story or account of an incident was written. Corbin refilled his coffee and rubbed his eyes in a preemptive measure to stave off the headache reading his pap's handwriting was going to bring. He began to read.

12.

July 3rd 1946

Saw Iness this afternoon. Came by while I was out in the top field plowing. Saw him standing there like a scarecrow, that mop of hair blowing from under his hat in the breeze. He had his arms wide and waving. I stopped the tractor and hopped down to see what the matter was.

"Mary is due in a week," he said, and there was a graveness in both his eyes and voice.

I nodded and knew why he felt as he did. Iness didn't give anything when it was his family's turn. A simple gift to show thanks was all we were ever asked for. One night in the end week of the month, a token was put out on the porch before you turned in. That act. That gesture is what kept the valley fruitful for us all. A basket of eggs or a bushel of spinach. A slab of roast or a jar of honey. That kept the black clouds from hovering over your house and all who dwell in it. These ain't rules we made; these are old ways. Old. Old. Old.

Inness said he forgot about the date; he had been busy fretting over Eileen's pregnancy, and Mary's for that matter.

'Ye can't forget,' I had told him then.

Now I patted him on the shoulder and told him it'd be fine. I reminded him of the incident with Eilieen, and assured him that had been the balance. The slate ought to be wiped now, and all accounts square. He tried to smile and said he hoped so. He was always a worrisome fellow; always. I watched him walk that long-legged walk of his down through the fields toward his truck along the road. I watched him, and tried not to remember that night in the barn them weeks ago. What the tearing of that cow's flesh sounded like when her birthing parts were ravaged. Didn't know a cow could scream. What seeing that long white thing was like, watching it slither from the pooling blood and fluids only to unfurl what looked to be a dozen long legs from itself. How it crawled too fast out into the night and disappeared into the tree line, where we saw it met by many other white shapes in the darkness. The sound of Iness's soft wailing over the death of his prized animal, and the gory mess on the floor of his barn. But most likely out of the fear that it was his mistake that caused it. I tried not to remember any of that. But I did. My God, I did.

13.

Corbin dropped the front cover of the notebook onto his hand, closing it, but also marking his place. He shook his head and emptied the mug beside him.

"What the Wicker Man fuck did I just read?"

The words were meant to be humorous, but there was little of it in them. Feeling as though he weren't alone, he turned quickly to the stove against the wall and the dark doorway of the living room. He heard a tap at the window, and spun back to face it. Nothing greeted him but the orange bleeding of the setting sun. He stood and flipped on the porch light. Nothing fled or moved. The branches of the tree by the old outhouse seemed to wave, yet the high grass remained still. He stared for uncomfortable minutes before deciding to get some work done. Ignoring the notebooks on the chipped wooden table, Corbin made his way into the room between the kitchen and the living room—if you went through the other doorway, the pattern of rooms made a circle. Kitchen to living room to store room/middle room (as they referred to it) back to kitchen, or reversed if you went that way. He stood and looked at the stacks of stuff. Boxes of linens, curtains and tablecloths. Many still in packaging, unused. Tied bundles of newspapers and magazines. There were seven brooms leaning in the corner, two well used and the other five brand new. The light from the ceiling fixture glowed hazy through a thick cobweb cowl. Corbin sighed and grabbed a broom to whisk away the dimming web and see if it would improve the illumination. It did, only slightly. He began grabbing bundles of papers and carried them out through the side door to the waiting sun room. For some reason, fingers of unease walked his spine and he was as quick to get back inside as the sun was to hide behind the mountain and let the moon sit in its place for a while.

14.

The kitchen was fogged with smoke from the four cigarettes he'd smoked while eating the second sandwich he'd brought. His provisions had been sparse. A box of cereal and a half gallon of milk, three pre-made sandwiches and a pack of rolls, cheese slices and bologna. A bag of pretzels and a gallon of water. Mike had insisted on paying for it, and Corbin hardly argued.

He picked up the red notebook and opened it. He considered another cigarette before he started reading, but decided to wait. He figured his lungs were thankful.

July 17th, 1946

The rain finally let up, stopped for the day, but bein' Thursday, I know it's coming back for a few more days. It's the way. On and on.

The crops drank it up quick and were happy to do it, from the gloaty look of 'em. I went to see Iness and his wife. She oughta be due any time now. He's scared as hell and if I'm honest he may ought be. He forgot his tithe two months ago, and last month his cow and her calf was taken to reckon it. He worries that ain't enough. Frets that Mary or the baby might be marked. I told him he's just being a nervous Nellie . . . but is he? I mean, I don't know. I never know'd much about this stuff. Just what my Pa told me as his told him. The valley is old and we were far from the first to live here. That what was here first never left, just slid aside to give us a berth. 'Us' being the tribes what lived here before the white men came and forced them off under the guise of helping them out. Bastards we are. Pa always said of the Air of the Valley, that's what he called it. That we got to be thankful and show our appreciation. That's how Pa put it. It seemed hard to believe until I was older and began to see the patterns and lines in things, as they were. Cycles. The middle week of the month always brought rain here, regardless of the forecast or almanac or anything. Even if you were to drive out of the valley, once you broached the mountain and started down the other side, clear blue sky would be waitin' for ya. A week of rain. Heavy or light, could be counted upon in the valley, letting us know it was halfway to offering. Sounds crazy as I'm readin' it but it is so.

I'll go out and feed the dog and put some water and food down for the barn cats during the break in the rain. I'll do that. That's what I'll do.

⁕

July 28th, 1946

I thought Iness was going to pound the damn door off its hinges. Evelyn was just starting dinner when he came. Peeling potatoes, I think. I opened the door and asked what the hell the matter was. His face was chalk white and he said it were time. Mary was in labor. I looked at my wife and she grimly nodded. I grabbed my hat and coat and stepped out onto the porch with Iness.

"You walked here?" I asked, since I didn't see his truck nowhere.

He nodded. Said it wouldn't turn over.

I sighed and grabbed his sleeve, pulled him to the barn where I had my truck. I had to kick one of the chickens outta the wheel well, but we were on our way in no time. Iness was practically on the verge of a conniption it looked like, and his eyes were so wide. The man was terrified. I had nothing to say that could help so I just patted him on the shoulder. I don't think it helped at all.

The trees blurred by as I tore down the dirt road as quick as I could. The rain got heavier and I could hardly see. The wipers trying to keep up with the downpour was like trying to carry water in a sieve, but I let them go. The rhythm of them, somehow slightly soothing. We rounded the bend and I saw the little farm off to the right. A small house with a middlin' barn across from it. We stopped in front of the barn and Iness jumped out before I'd even set the brake.

"Come on, hurry."

His voice was unraveling, like his mind if'n you ask me, but I did as he told me to.

The house was dark and quiet. He ran room to room hollering for his wife and no voice called out in return. I felt itchy under my skin. Something was not right, not at all. Iness came back and looked at me.

"Let's check the barn," he says.

I shrug. Thinking to myself, 'Why would a woman having a baby go to the barn in the blasted rain?' But what do I know about anything?

Mary was in the barn. She was laying on her back in a pile of straw. The glow of the lantern she must've carried out spattered feeble light over the scene. There were feathers floating in the air like snow. Gathered around her, in an image almost outta the Bible, were several cows and sheep. Knelt down, they silently stared at the woman. She had her house dress hiked up to her waist, they could see her naked lower half, shiny with sweat. I looked at Iness, partly embarrassed and partly scared.

"Get her up and to the car. Now!" I shouted.

Seemed to be the thing to do. I grabbed her left side and Iness her right and we got her standing. He pulled her dress down to cover her nudity. I noted that there was blood marking the hem of her dress and running down her thighs. We were getting short on time. He barely had the door closed before we tore out of the driveway. The night bit down darker in front of us, but I drove like a bat out of hell. I kept my foot down until I made the end and saw the water covering the road before the bridge. The bridge was underwater as well. I stopped the truck and looked at Iness and then at Mary. She was panting like a dog and I swear I could see the baby moving under the flesh of her belly. The skin bulged and rippled. I swallowed hard and looked at the road behind us. The river was beginning to lick at it as well. We needed to make a move.

"Iness . . . " I said.

"Go back," he said, but mumbled it.

I swung us around and we went back to their house. The river ate the road behind us as we went, me watching it in the rearview mirror. As weird as shit in the valley had always been—the stories I had heard over the years, the things I had seen with my own eyes—this was the first time I ever felt truly in danger and afraid of what was there. I just nodded and drove until I saw the small farm come into view again. I eased to a stop right by the porch, and yanked the brake.

"Get her in," I said as I hopped out and ran around to help.

The poor woman seemed almost unconscious, her head fell forward and her tongue hung from her lips. It looked like a small gray slug. Her eyes were slits with only white visible. My skin crawled.

"Move, Iness!"

He did. We both did. The woman's feet barely touched the ground; her toes gouged furrows in the gravel of the path to the porch. The rainfall softened but did not stop. The moon scowled behind the night clouds.

Bad signs were by the bushel that night.

The lights we'd left on when we initially left were off now. The rooms were obstacle courses of low tables and high-back chairs. Bookcases lined the walls and the splinters of moonlight that made it through the windows and reflected in the glass of their doors, gave away their location. I nearly fell over a hassock as I lifted Mary's legs and put her on the couch. Iness hefted her shoulders, and we got her laid out. I found a pillow and eased it under her head. A groan fell from her lips, wormy and wet. Iness stared at her. His lips moved, almost like in spasm, but the words were very soft. I listened in the uneasy quiet. He was praying. I looked away in shame. I caught movement at the window beside the sofa and saw the cows from the barn, their large noses pressed against the glass. No steam from their breath. Their eyes were shining and black. My skin danced, as did my guts.

"Iness, we can't get her to town. The doctor can't get here either."

I wrinkled my nose at the tang of the thick blood that marked her pale legs. What was earlier a thin trickling was now a pulsing flow. It dripped from her ankles onto the wooden floor. I watched it disappear between the boards, I imagined I heard a lapping sound. I screamed inside my head to stay focused.

"Iness. Something is wrong."

I'd delivered enough calves and kids over the years to know what to look for, and what I saw there was chillingly wrong. She oughta have been more ready.

I ran to the kitchen and washed my hands quickly, and returned to my hunker by the couch. I closed my eyes and exhaled a silent prayer as I slid my fingers into her. I'm no doctor, not even a veterinarian. I've learned to help stock with birthin' outta necessity and seclusion. Now, Mary, she was swole, which seemed right. But there was no dilation, the only wetness came from the bleeding, it was too thick, too heavy. I worked my hand up to my thumb, and heard Mary gasp. I looked to see her smiling, her eyes rolled up and white as wool. Something grazed the tips of my fingers. Something hard and rough. It felt like beef tongue. Something nipped at my fingers. I yanked my hand away. Mary's eyes fluttered at the suddenness of the action. Iness stared at my hand, slicked in blackish red.

"Iness, the baby isn't right. I fear it won't survive, but I'll need to take it to save your wife."

"My son," was all the poor man spoke. A whisper so loud it hurt my heart and ears.

I looked at him, shaking my head. "I don't think . . . "

"My son," he said again, and squeezed his wife's hand tightly. I heard bones crackle. Mary never made a peep. Her chest still.

I took a deep breath and slid my hand once more into her, far as I could, until my fingers grazed what felt like the heel of a foot.

"My God, Iness, he's breech."

Iness kept his head down, held Mary's cooling hand against his lips that were still leaking prayers.

I closed my fingers around what felt like a foot. My fingers moved slightly, feeling for toes that weren't there. Maybe out of reach. I gritted my teeth and began to slowly pull. The slow pulse of blood from her loins grew angrier, and loudly pattered against the floor by my knees. The smell was unreal. Warm blood reek mixed with another, headier smell. Darkly sour but sweet . . . reminded me of silage. I had my hand nearly clear when a sudden move inside her caused me to lose my grip. A small white thing began to crown. I looked at Iness. Maybe I'd been wrong. This was the head after all. As it came out further, I realized how both horribly right and wrong I was. And as the long white thing that slid from my friend's wife opened an impossible jaw to show a row of spindly teeth, I opened my mouth and let loose with a scream that echoed through the farmhouse. Iness reached for the thing and I batted his hand away. It wriggled free of its mother with force enough to further tear the flesh around. More dark blood flowed. Mary groaned and fell still as Iness, again, reached for the thing.

"Ain't no son of yours," I said, and raised a thick boot over the abomination that squirmed on the floor in a puddle of Mary's blood. It looked like a large tadpole, with several small appendages tucked under it, not yet free from the mucous webbing that semi-bound it. It looked at me with reddish eyes that dotted the flesh about that damned mouth. It squealed like a piglet and I brought my foot down, hard as I could. The sound of that head busting was like a pumpkin under the plow. Iness screamed and pushed me to the floor. His eyes wild, his mouth a ragged snarling thing. I put my hands up and pushed back at the same time, catching the man off balance. He stumbled backwards and over the coffee table, falling to the floor. His head hit the edge of the hearth with a wet thunk. The room was quiet then. I stood and looked at the horror around me. My friend and neighbor on the floor, his skull cracked and what was in it peeking through. His wife dead on the sofa, coated with her own blood. And on the floor by my feet, the remains of the monster she bore.

I looked out the window, and the animals were still there, gaping, wide eyed and, my God, smiling. It was only then that I realized for them to be peeking in that window, they must be standing upright as a man. My spine danced and I think my bowels loosed some. I made for the door. I heard a cacophony of animal noises outside, mixing with the drone of the falling rain. I heard a slurping sound and saw another creature slip from dead Mary's womb, and as I watched it writhe next to its dead brother, another slipped through. By the time a fourth hit the floor, I was at the door. I shoved it open and ran for the truck. Opening the door and jumping in without a look back. I sat in it for long minutes and with unbelieving eyes, watched as the cows and goats and pigs, in impossible pairs, walked into the house on two legs like people. The glow from their eyes like fireflies.

I slowly got out and went to the shed by the barn. I grabbed the cans of fuel mix from the table and jogged to the house. I snuck a peek in the window and watched as the cow lay atop the dead woman, the white creatures suckling from udders unfull. Trickles of red fled from the sucking mouths. I poured the cans around the house. Splashing up the boards that made the walls. I emptied them both and stood back. The lighter in my pocket had been my father's, and were I to ever have a son, I hoped it to be his. I flicked the wheel and even in the damp air and slight drizzle, a flame erupted. I leaned in, let it kiss the gas and oil-slicked wood. It bloomed into flames that ran along the side of the house. I swiftly walked backwards to the truck, listening to the screams from inside the burning structure. I closed my eyes as I heard the low cries of the farm stock, but also the high screams of a woman. I heard crying babies and I heard whispers threaded through it all. The fire licked at the roof, and the windows bent and broke in the fever of the blaze.

And then I heard laughter. I think that it may have been coming from me.

15.

Corbin closed the notebook. The sweat that wet his forehead dripped onto the table and the backs of his hands. He looked up at the clock, seeing there was no light outside. Nine forty-five. He exhaled heavily and groaned as he stood from the table. He felt uncomfortable now. 'Shaken' might be a better word. He stared at the notebooks again, and his stomach rolled.

"Maybe Pap fancied himself a writer. Maybe that's a manuscript?" He tried to rationalize to himself, but he wasn't buying it.

Corbin looked out the window above the sink and saw the forest line in the dark of night. The silhouette of the trees looked darker than the night sky beyond, like it could have been roughly cut from construction paper. He saw movement near the edge of the field, thought he caught white shapes that seemed to bounce and leap in the low brush that bordered the pasture. He heard the call of some animal closer to the house—probably a coyote or a fox in the side garden. Corbin turned on the porch light and made sure the door was locked by both chain and deadbolt.

Because that would definitely keep an ancient woodland pagan evil at bay, wouldn't it?

Corbin stared out the window and saw no movement, heard no

more noises. He kept watch for several more minutes before he went into the living room, leaving the light on in the kitchen—never noticing the small, masked face of the racoon, Cheshire-cat grinning through the window above the sink. Its button black eyes twinkled like stars.

16.

Corbin sat in his grandfather's old recliner. He allowed his fingers to explore the cracks in the Naugahyde that had been taped long ago. The curled edges were devoid of stickiness. He looked to the bookshelf by the chair, clotted with old paperback editions of westerns. He glanced down and saw one of the man's homemade spittoons: a large coffee can, a murky pond of brown spit covering the bottom. He grimaced.

Gross, Pap. Just gross.

He heard a sound above his head like footsteps. Several at both ends of the ceiling. He bit his lip. "Has to be squirrels and bats having a hoedown," he mumbled to himself.

He reached for a copy of *Last of the Plainsman,* when the noises above grew to what sounded like stomping. He froze and listened hard. Were there voices? The squeaking thrum was still going on, almost rhythmic. Was that someone giggling? He heard a dull thump from across the room and looked to the window behind the television. He thought he saw a smear of pale move away quickly.

"Right," he announced to himself, and stood up. He went back into the kitchen and sat at the table. He looked at the red notebook and decided he'd maybe had enough of that one for now. He'd check out the account book for a little while, let the columns of names and numbers calm his obviously over-stimulated nerves and imagination.

It took less than half an hour to read through the accounts. They filled nearly half of the pages. The rest were indecipherable scribbles, and a page that looked like some sort of map which vaguely resembled the farm's acreage. There were a couple of discrepancies: a creek or stream that ran between the house and the barn, and what seemed to be a cave or something right next to the house on the westerly side. It almost looked like a beehive as a child would have rendered it. He pursed his lips and closed that book, as doing so the light caught a very small notation at the bottom corner of the page. He lifted the thick board cover and tilted the page to the light. The word was in faded pencil, visible only in the perfect slant of light—and even then, barely. It was a date. 1748.

Corbin found himself frowning. That would predate the house and buildings by well over a century. Perhaps the number meant something else. He shut it and opened the red book. The wind was picking up outside, and he tried to pay its moan no mind. He flipped back to the beginning, before all the nightmare fuel of the later passages began.

17.

Not sure why I decided to write this all down. I'll never leave the valley, and I suspect any kin I may have that had the sense to leave won't be coming back of their own mind. My pa always told me the valley would be mine one day—not all of it, but the farm and all the land that went with it. He told me of the ways and duties of life there. How they would sound so very mad but that, in truth, they're very simple and obliging both ways if followed. Thinking about the things he told me, the pieces I gathered on my own and stuck to over the years since, I'm not exactly sure why I allowed myself to be shackled here as well.

He spoke of the woods and the 'Kin' that lived there. Called them the 'Kin', as he said they were as veins that connected us to the land and nature. They had always been there and could be kind if of a mind to be. He said they were sometimes thin and long, grub white and leggy. They scampered in trees and flitted through the air in the night. He told me only then. I asked what happened to them in the daylight and he made a sad face, almost as a scolded child would, and said: "Kin that be caught in the teeth of the sun, hang there and shrivel. They die and become food for the birds and things. Tallow."

I wasn't sure about swallowing this. I could almost see the hook.

He patted my shoulder and promised me it was true, and it was simple. A set upon time of offering and tithe was agreed upon many years ago by the first settlers of the valley. The original tribes. As they died off, more and more tales and truths were passed on to those first farmers who came here. Simple sacrifices. Things of use freely given, they called it. A basket of eggs, a crock of honey or butter, a string of smoked fish. Offerings put on the cusp of your domain, and with no exceptions or expectations. In return the valley would sing to ye, croon with sunshine and lullaby with sweet rain when the ground thirsted. An army of worms to turn deep down and awaken the soil. Warmth when it was cold. The valley would provide, but lest ye not take it for granted, always be watching and listening. The Kin keep marks, boy.

"Do the things of the valley eat eggs and fish?" I had asked, probably foolish.

Pa smirked and patted my dirty cheek.

"They eat what they long to. But like any gift, my boy, it's the thought that counts."

We began to walk to the barn, stopping between it and the house. Pa knelt and put a hand to the dirt of the lane that ran from the river trail to the road between the fields and the house. Not paved, but worn by use.

"This is the river," he said, "where it started before it slid beneath to where it is now. Like a mother whose child is near. Listen and you can hear her rushing still. Go on."

And I did. I put my ear to the pebbled and dusty ground and I could hear the whisper of moving water. I could smell the mud and feel it between my fingers. Very old things wriggled there. I looked at Pa, and he was smiling.

"From there springs everything, my boy. Everything."

I just nodded, my head too full and swimming for much else.

18.

By the end of that month, Pa was dead. He had been working in the small field beside the house when he plowed into a nest of hornets and was stung to death. I found him as I was coming from school. I usually cut through that garden as a shortcut. I swung my books and was daydreaming when I heard the buzzing hum. It sounded like a tuning fork we had at school. Made my teeth feel the same. I saw the plow unmanned, and saw what looked like a shadow sliding around in the air around it. I got closer and saw Pa on his knees, leaning forward with his forehead to the earth. He was covered in welts and his lips were swollen. His eyes had disappeared in puffed pockets of flesh. I dropped my books and ran to the house. I called for Mama. She was in the living room, in her rocking chair. The clicking of her needles, the only sound in the room. Her eyes were wet and I saw trails from earlier tears on her cheeks. I could only manage a single word: "Pa."

My mother nodded and put down her yarn. She pulled me close and held me and all I could make out from the sobbing gibberish she spewed into my neck was: "Sometimes we don't have a say."

She spoke not another word the rest of that day or the ones after. She went back to her knitting and I watched out the window as Old and Young Ken Hughes came in their wagon. I peered through a daze as they carried my pa to the back of the buckboard and laid him across its slats, a bed of linen and burlap beneath him and a quilt pulled over his face. I had nightmares of the image of my father's swollen hand, his arm bouncing loose where it dangled over the back of the wagon as the men headed to the road to town.

I thought about what my ma had said again, and I didn't know what she meant then—but I did later. The valley was a cage. And while we were led to believe that we made the choice and we picked the offerings, once in a while, the Kin made their own choice: one wrapped in heartache and grief. Left us to shake the bars and holler while they just carried on with their dark doings.

19.

Corbin flipped a few pages before he started reading again.

I saw them tonight, just after dusk: the Kin as hornets. When my pa died all those years ago, the neighbors came back from taking his body, intent on dousing the nest and burning out the bastards. Problem was there weren't any nests to be found. The earth around where my father had been felled was just packed dirt, except where furrowed for garden crop. The men's faces were drawn as they put the cans back on the wagon bed and left without a word. My ma just stood at the edge of the porch, watching them go.

That was the last I had thought of hornets, until tonight.

It was after dinner, and Evelyn was in her spot at the table, reading her wretched papers. I went out for a smoke. Generally I'm a chewer, but once in a while I like the pipe, and the weather was kindly. I stood out there and smoked when I heard the buzzing. It was low and worked like a splinter under the skin. I felt it as well as heard it, dancing along my spine. It sounded electric. I stepped off the porch and around to the side of the house where the garden lived. The same patch where my pa was felled. Now, I assure you, I have been on this farm and valley my entire life, and until this evening had never seen this. I mean, I have witnessed the madness of the Kin in many guises and shapes, but this particular vision was fresh. To me.

The fading sun was far enough that the shadows were starting to become brazen, wrapping their dark arms around the valley. I walked towards the garden, and as I got to the edge the mixture of dying sunlight and wobbling shadow intersected in such a manner as to illuminate something. I'm not sure how to go on . . . it was a hive. Right in the garden, but not actually in the garden. The garden was untouched, even though the large nest was in the same space. I'd say they were in different sheets of being. I'm not a smart man, by book or education, but I know what I know and I think this was a bit of the Kin world showing through a thin-skinned place. Like the surface of an eye.

It was about the size of a modest shed. Ribbed and smooth, yet the texture looked pebbled in some way. It shimmered. There was a mouth like that of a cave near the side closest to the house, and from it were emerging what could only be bumblebees, not hornets. But some otherworldly interpretation of them. They were the size of small rabbits, and transparent. They bobbed and floated clumsily around the nest. Their eyes were bulging and resembled those of a man. They had mannish mouths that chittered with thick teeth that were like quills or needles. Their legs hung beneath them, tipped with small hands and thin fingers. I stood still so as to not draw their attention. They seemed to pay me no mind. I heard a sound, and saw one of the barn cats standing by the porch steps. The poor creature's gold fur was raised, its tail puffed. A low growl came from its throat. One of the flying creatures noticed it. And its eyes widened. A whine fell from its horrible mouth as it flew at the cat, spinning around as it did so, presenting the long stinger and its vicious barb. The cat hissed and the bee-thing speared it with its tail. The stinger, though seeming unsolid as the creature that bore it, impaled the poor cat—which then screamed like a baby. The bee-thing slowly rose, carrying the weight of the dying animal on its stinger. It flew to the hive, and disappeared through the mouth. A few other bees lit on the ground and lapped up the blood lost from the cat. I didn't move. I couldn't. I watched as the entire vision faded with the last rays of the sun and the assertion of total darkness. When the hive was gone, having faded in the darkness, I began hearing the things of the woods. Screeching and calling to one another in their way. Only then did I creep inside and lock the doors and windows and spend the bulk of the night wary and weary, watching the swatches of white cavort in the dark shadows of the forest and fields.

20.

It began as beginnings often do: with a birth of sorts. The spring that flowed from the cleft at the base of the mountain, up at the edge of the topmost field. The edges of the cleft tufted with moss, giving it an almost obscene appearance. The waters that flowed from it fed the earth and spread downward and outward across the valley. Our valley. The place is strange yet good. Queer in its oldness and it unafearedness. The animals here are bold. Foxes stare you down at dusk and rabbits watch with unnerving tether. The air is oh so sweet, and always as such. The water also. There is strangeness all around this place, slight or bludgeoning. There are rains, and sometimes they are of the normal water variety— while others have been a deluge of snails or wriggling things. One time a rain of meat fell, landing only on that top pasture. Small, nearly cubed pieces of red flesh that were set upon by a murder of crows so large that when they lit out from the hedging woods, it looked as premature nightfall. However odd the place is, we have settled and stitched ourselves here. Anchor laid by my father and others many years ago. The farm and the duties left to me by my father, as left to him by his, and I shall pass them on to mine, and pray he shall likewise do the same with his, and onward. I can hear the trees murmuring now, and the air is drooling with the promise of rain. Saliva wetting a mouth for an offering feast.

⚉

Corbin noted a difference in the handwriting, and saw that the section was from a letter which had been carefully trimmed and pasted onto the page of the notebook. He saw the footnote accrediting the text to Legam Worthy, dated 1877, only when he prepared to turn the page.

21.

There have been some troubling events as of recent. The rains have lasted longer than usual. Usually the middle week of the month, but now we're four days beyond that and still the sky spits on us. The ground is sogged. I fear it might be a punishment of some sort—for the poor offering from the Eichelbergers. Their prized sow birthed a litter of piglets the Sunday of tithe week, and two of them were stillborn, pink as babies and perfect save for the fact they had no eyes. Just smooth skin where they should have been. Wilmer put them out in front of his buckboard—I don't wager on purpose, but just thinking to get rid of them the next day. But damn the date. He never noticed it and the following morning the rains began. Black as soot and smelling sour. There came a low moaning from the woods around the valley. In the barns, the animals cowered. A worm turned on that day . . .

. . . we lost old man Kreider last night. He'd gone mad, they said. They, always they. They: the others who live in the valley. I often see them act as one. Fingers on an unseen hand. Kreider had tried to burn down his barn. He cut the throats of all his animals. Piled them in front of the house. The blood pooled in the ruts and pockets of the property. When the first neighbors arrived, they found him rutting with a tree at the edge of his field. He thrust into it with reckless fervor, they said, and had to be pulled away from it. His roger was bleeding and raw yet he had completed his vile deed, as they said the knothole in the tree wept his seed. They dragged the old man back to the barn, which was now only smoldering as the others had managed to snuff out the flames. Kreider's eyes had gone white and he slobbered gibberish. As they tried to get him into their wagon, he broke free and ran, managing to kick one of the young men who held him. The crazed fellow disappeared into the woods. They heard his wild laughter well into the night.

The following morning, a search party was assembled to scour the entirety of the valley. No trace of the old man was ever found. They did report that the tree the man had . . . befouled . . . was also gone. A ragged hole in the earth was all that marked its existence.—Legam, 1880

22.

August 3rd, 2003

There's a line, has to be. A thick thread that sews history, that sutures years to years in a quilt of lineage and inheritance. A vein to feed the heart of recollection. A vine. And as with most vines, oftentimes pruning is a necessity. An anchoring bloodline, maybe? I cannot say why the Worthys were set upon . . . chosen . . . cursed to be the vein of the valley, but we were. My great grandfather and his wife were one of the first white families to settle the area. He was met by the head of the tribe that had called the woods and hills and mountain home. My great grandfather was given permission to tame the valley, but also warned that it was for good reason that they had avoided it. The valley was hungry, they told him. Those who lived there were strange and wily. They spoke of things that nature held no sway over. The warnings were shrugged off, as they usually are. And here we are. A hundred years and some change later, and I feel the thread is fraying for me. I have no one to pass the chore to, a chore that's been my family duty for a long, long time. My own children beat me to the finish line. Cancer or tragedy—I suppose they are synonymous. There is only one remaining, and I've not seen the boy in some time. He has a dower coming his way. I hope my letting him break the lead and run was enough to spare him. I wish I'd had the time or spine to have explained it in person . . .

23.

Shattering the silence of the farmhouse, a burst of laughter from upstairs, loud but muffled by floorboards. Corbin jumped and swore at the sudden intrusion. His heart raced and his breathing hitched. He quickly stood, and looked around the room. Just the boxes and bags of donations he'd assembled the last three days. He heard a thump from outside, and looked out the window. Only darkness returned his stare, a wall of black gauze dotted by shining pairs of dots. His skin danced at the realization that something . . . somethings were watching him back. He slid his phone from his pocket and scrolled for Mike's number, tapping it with his thumb once he found it. The ringing went unanswered. He disconnected and thumbed the number again. Nothing but a slight hiss of static, the sound like the pages of an old newspaper turning. He heard more muted laughter above, then footfalls. The steps were heavy, and there were too many to be from a single person. His heart beat faster, and his breathing followed. He found himself at the foot of the steps, looking up at the doors now illuminated by the beam of his phone light. The rope and sign that had fenced them closed was on the floor, under a layer of dust, as though they'd been down for years. Corbin heard voices. Squeaking, a pulsing beat. He swallowed something slick in his throat and took a deep breath. He started up. He felt the knob beneath his fingers before he realized he'd cleared the staircase already. The knob was vibrating like a tuning fork. He clenched his teeth and closed his eyes. There was a click as he turned it, and, as though it weighed a ton, he slowly pushed it open.

24.

Corbin stood at the threshold. In stark contrast to the sight before him, his brain whispered that his great grandfather had carried his great grandmother across this very spot so many decades ago. He shook his head and raised his hand, wielding the phone light. When the thin beam hit the far corner of the room, the sounds grew as though someone were thumbing an invisible volume knob somewhere. The squeaking that had been almost subliminal the past few days was loud and sharp. It stabbed into his ears like an awl. He couldn't quite process what he saw.

The corner—all of it, floor to ceiling—was a pulsing, furred mass. Mottled gray and dark bursts of fur and leathery wings that flailed and shook. There were eyes, thousands of them, all twinkling in the light of his phone. There were teeth in the tiny mouths that squealed and shrieked. They were somehow as one, grown together in an enormous thing that filled the end of the room. The bulk pulsed . . . beat like a huge heart. The wings that touched the walls had become one with the wood and plaster; their thick veins bulged and rivulets of blood ran from beneath the pictures that hung on them. The nail holes from long, long ago acted as still-fresh wounds.

Corbin saw movement in the shadows to his left and showed

the light there. He shook his head and tried to speak. "No," was all he could manage, as the bright rope of light shone on the face of his great grandmother, and then across all the relatives he'd seen buried. There were faces he had seen at work as well. They all smiled and nodded at him. Their skin, waxy and wet. He took a step backward, out onto the landing. The heart of the house beat louder, and with each one, the floor shook. Corbin looked back over his shoulder from the landing and saw his pap standing on the stairs, with things low and furred behind him. Things with eyes that twinkled and smiled. The old man wore a dour expression. Sad, hooded eyes that stared at the floor while he slowly shook his head. He looked up, into the wide eyes of his great-grandson.

"I wish you'd listened, boy."

Corbin held up a hand..

The old man held out his other and in it he held the notebooks. "Yours now."

"This can't be. I'm dreaming again. I've fallen or had a stroke . . . "

Anger or annoyance sprouted in the old man's features. He grimaced and spoke in a voice that was as commanding and rich in death as before.

"Boy, some people don't even have families. Some folks live their entire lives without knowing the honor of doing for others. You—you had that. You were given a very special place in this world. And you threw it away. I thought I . . . I . . . it weren't. They. *They* gave you an offering, and you took it, and then just like that, you crumpled it up and tossed it over your shoulder. You were given a special out, Corbin. I made a special arrangement to keep you from having to wear the thorny crown here, this millstone of a valley. But you pissed on it. A simple act of disobedience damns ye, and well . . . here we are." The old man hung his head in shame, red tears streaming down gaunt, pale cheeks.

Corbin could articulate no response. He pushed by his pap and ran down the steps, tripping over possums and rabbits and the other creatures that clogged the passageway. He made it to the front door and threw it open. The night air was full of activity. Translucent bees bobbed in the thin mist, looking just as described in the notes. He saw pale ghosts of fish swimming through the currents of the night. He saw white shapes in the woods. So many of them. He looked at the fat moon and wished it to be the sun, to turn all these nightmares into tallow and fill the bellies of birds.

He was still wishing when he got to the shed, and the waiting gas cans. He stuffed the notebooks down the front of his jeans and grabbed the tins of fuel. He wept quietly as he turned and went back towards the house.

A minute later the lights went out. Seconds after that, Corbin made new light. He stood until it began to chew up the ancient farmhouse. Its orange glow nipped at the night.

25.

Corbin sat on the chair in the service station. His legs were still shaking from both the strange events he'd endured, and from running for nine miles out of the valley and to the main road. He shifted the blanket and pulled the notebooks from under his waistband. He frowned and felt tears again as he looked at his inheritance. Old paper and spiral wire. Words in pencil. He watched the television on the back counter and read the ticker, since the volume was too low for him to hear. The image was of hungry flames swallowing forest and field. A house reduced to smoldering wood and melted glass. The fire started at a farm and spread the entire valley. Uncanny, given the recent rains. The fireman who was speaking looked surprised. Corbin closed his eyes.

26.

Six Months Later

"Darla, I'm going to take Mrs Hendrickson out for some night air. She asked and I think she's fine for it."

"Okay, Corbin. Hildegarde could use it. I also assume you want a smoke, yeah?"

"I cannot tell a lie."

The pair chuckled, and Corbin went down the hall. He returned back pushing the old woman in her chair. Her hair was thin and white, her enormous glasses worthless for anything other than amplifying the marbled cataracts on her eyes. Her thin hands gripped the armrest and she hollered: "Wheee!" as she was pushed down the hallway.

Darla smiled and ducked back to her paperwork. Corbin and old Hildegarde turned the corner in the direction of the side exit. Corbin opened the door and swiveled the chair onto the concrete of the patio. He stepped out and looked around at the shadows of the tree line behind the home. The moon was just showing its face over the edge of the mountain, like Kilroy. He rolled Hildegarde to the edge of the cement and locked the brake on her wheels. He took a deep breath and looked down at her smiling face.

"Let me get you a blanket, Mrs H. It might be chilly for you. Be right back."

She nodded and smiled as she looked at the woods, most likely seeing them more out of memory than in reality. Corbin went back into the building and stopped just inside the door. He turned the lock and peered out the window, his eyes squinting to keep the tears back. He saw the first white shapes high up the tree line, nearer the base of the mountain—but then more cropped up, moving closer with terrifying speed. He saw the thin legs and arms puncturing the shadows as they ran for the old woman. Watched them swarm over her in a plaid tide, static devouring a solid image. It happened in silence. The slight rush of the evening breeze was enough to mask their movement as they flowed back into the woods. Corbin wished he'd waited until after his cigarette. He pushed the empty chair back inside and returned it to the store room. He informed Darla that Mrs Hendrickson had enjoyed her fresh air and was now sleeping soundly in her room; that he had gotten a call earlier from her grandson that they were coming to get her in the morning to take her home for her final days. He said he had forgotten to tell her with all that's on his mind these days. Corbin went into the small staff washroom and scrubbed his hands. He brushed them until the skin was bright pink and stinging, and the steam on the mirror rendered his tears invisible.

THE END?

Not if you want to dive into more of Crystal Lake Publishing's Tales from the Darkest Depths!

Check out our amazing website and online store.
https://www.crystallakepub.com

We always have great new projects and content on the website to dive into, as well as a newsletter, behind the scenes options, social media platforms, our own dark fiction shared-world series and our very own webstore. If you use the IGotMyCLPBook! coupon code in the store (at the checkout), you'll get a one-time-only 50% discount on your first eBook purchase!

Our webstore even has categories specifically for KU books, non-fiction, anthologies, and of course more novels and novellas.

Subscribe to Crystal Lake Publishing's Dark Tide series for updates, specials, behind-the-scenes content, and a special selection of bonus stories - http://eepurl.com/hKVGkr

ABOUT THE AUTHORS

Chad Lutzke has written for Famous Monsters of Filmland, Rue Morgue, Cemetery Dance, and Scream magazine. His short fiction can be found in several dozen magazines and anthologies, and some of his books include: *Of Foster Homes & Flies, Stirring the Sheets, Cannibal Creator, Skullface Boy, The Same Deep Water as You,* and The Neon Own series. Lutzke's work has been praised by authors Jack Ketchum, Richard Chizmar, Joe R. Lansdale, Stephen Graham Jones, Tim Waggoner, and his own mother. He can be found lurking the internet at www.chadlutzke.com

Robert Ford has written the novels *The Compound, Dead Pennies, No Lipstick in Avalon,* and the novellas *Samson and Denial, Ring of Fire, The Last Firefly of Summer, Bordertown,* and *Big Stakes Jackie.* He has also written a supernatural western, *Blood Roses,* and *The God Beneath my Garden,* a collection of his short fiction.

He has co-authored the novella *Rattlesnake Kisses,* and *Cattywampus* with John Boden.

He can confirm the grass actually *is* greener on the other side, but it's only because of the bodies buried there.

You can find out more about what he's up to by visiting robertfordauthor.com

John Boden lives with his beautiful wife and two sons, in a house sweetly haunted by the ghost of a beautician named, Darlene.

He likes collecting lots of things and won't usually shut up about it. His writing is fairly well received and has been called unique of style. His work has been published in the form of stories in several anthologies and as novellas.

He plays well with others as is evidenced by collaborative works with Mercedes M. Yardley, Bracken MacLeod, Kurt Newton, Brian Rosenberger, Chad Lutzke and Robert Ford.

He's easy to track down either on Facebook or Twitter (JohnBoden1970)

Crystal Lake Publishing's most popular anthologies:

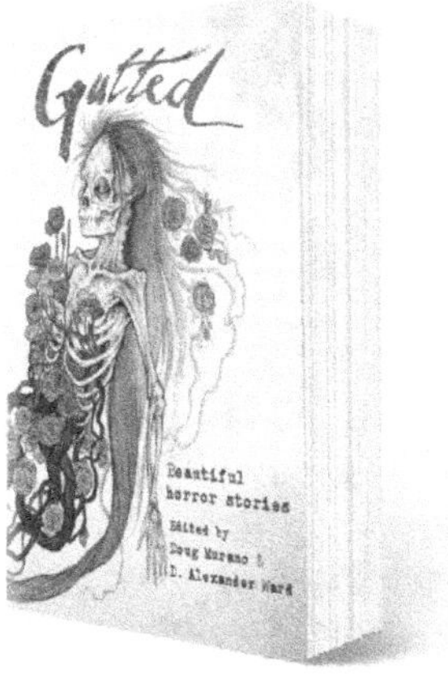

Readers . . .

Thank you for reading *Dark Tide Vol.1*. We hope you enjoyed this novel.

If you have a moment, please review *Dark Tide Vol. 1* at the store where you bought it.

Help other readers by telling them why you enjoyed this book. No need to write an in-depth discussion. Even a single sentence will be greatly appreciated. Reviews go a long way to helping a book sell, and is great for an author's career. It'll also help us to continue publishing quality books. You can also share a photo of yourself holding this book with the hashtag #IGotMyCLPBook!

Thank you again for taking the time to journey with Crystal Lake Publishing.

Visit our Linktree page for a list of our social media platforms.
https://linktr.ee/CrystalLakePublishing

Our Mission Statement:

Since its founding in August 2012, Crystal Lake Publishing has quickly become one of the world's leading publishers of Dark Fiction and Horror books in print, eBook, and audio formats.

While we strive to present only the highest quality fiction and entertainment, we also endeavour to support authors along their writing journey. We offer our time and experience in non-fiction projects, as well as author mentoring and services, at competitive prices.

With several Bram Stoker Award wins and many other wins and nominations (including the HWA's Specialty Press Award), Crystal Lake Publishing puts integrity, honor, and respect at the forefront of our publishing operations.

We strive for each book and outreach program we spearhead to not only entertain and touch or comment on issues that affect our readers, but also to strengthen and support the Dark Fiction field and its authors.

Not only do we find and publish authors we believe are destined for greatness, but we strive to work with men and woman who endeavour to be decent human beings who care more for others than themselves, while still being hard working, driven, and passionate artists and storytellers.

Crystal Lake Publishing is and will always be a beacon of what passion and dedication, combined with overwhelming teamwork and respect, can accomplish. We endeavour to know each and every one of our readers, while building personal relationships with our authors, reviewers, bloggers, podcasters, bookstores, and libraries.

We will be as trustworthy, forthright, and transparent as any business can be, while also keeping most of the headaches away from our authors, since it's our job to solve the problems so they can stay in a creative mind. Which of course also means paying our authors.

We do not just publish books, we present to you worlds within your world, doors within your mind, from talented authors who sacrifice so much for a moment of your time.

There are some amazing small presses out there, and through collaboration and open forums we will continue to support other presses in the goal of helping authors and showing the world what quality small presses are capable of accomplishing. No one wins when a small press goes down, so we will always be there to support hardworking, legitimate presses and their authors. We don't see Crystal Lake as the best press out there, but we will always strive to be the best, strive to be the most interactive and grateful, and even blessed press around. No matter what happens over time, we will also take our mission very seriously while appreciating where we are and enjoying the journey.

What do we offer our authors that they can't do for themselves through self-publishing?

We are big supporters of self-publishing (especially hybrid publishing), if done with care, patience, and planning. However, not every author has the time or inclination to do market research, advertise, and set up book launch strategies. Although a lot of authors are successful in doing it all, strong small presses will always be there for the authors who just want to do what they do best: write.

What we offer is experience, industry knowledge, contacts and trust built up over years. And due to our strong brand and trusting fanbase, every Crystal Lake Publishing book comes with weight of respect. In time our fans begin to trust our judgment and will try a new author purely based on our support of said author.

With each launch we strive to fine-tune our approach, learn from our mistakes, and increase our reach. We continue to assure our authors that we're here for them and that we'll carry the weight of the launch and dealing with third parties while they focus on their strengths—be it writing, interviews, blogs, signings, etc.

We also offer several mentoring packages to authors that include knowledge and skills they can use in both traditional and self-publishing endeavours.

We look forward to launching many new careers.

This is what we believe in. What we stand for. This will be our legacy.

Welcome to Crystal Lake Publishing— Tales from the Darkest Depths.